James Richard Joy, John Heyl Vincent

An Outline History of Rome

Volume 1

James Richard Joy, John Heyl Vincent

An Outline History of Rome
Volume 1

ISBN/EAN: 9783337381769

Printed in Europe, USA, Canada, Australia, Japan

Cover: Foto ©Andreas Hilbeck / pixelio.de

More available books at **www.hansebooks.com**

AN OUTLINE

HISTORY OF ROME

BY

JOHN H. VINCENT

AND

JAMES R. JOY

NEW YORK
CHAUTAUQUA PRESS
1889

The required books of the C. L. S. C. are recommended by a Council of Six. It must, however, be understood that recommendation does not involve an approval by the Council, or by any member of it, of every principle or doctrine contained in the book recommended.

PREFACE.

THE Hellenes, who settled the Grecian peninsula, and the Latins, who peopled Italy, were from the same old Indo-European stock. The former represented the literary and artistic power of the race, the latter its ruling energy. The one sounded the depth of philosophy, delighted in discussion, found inexhaustible sources of pleasure in public games and in the drama, transported the marble from Pentelicus to Athens, and transformed it into forms of grace and beauty; the other loved physical strength, the march and struggle and triumph of great armies, the building up of empire, the subjection of foreign powers, and the enactment and execution of laws for its own and for other people. The rulers proved more than a match for their elegant and cultured cousins. The sword was mightier than pen or chisel, and the Acropolis bowed to the Capitolinus. "First with the sword, and afterward with the more powerful arms of religious faith, Rome ruled a large portion of the European world for centuries."

The history of this great empire is especially interesting to the Christian student. While Ahaz ruled in

Judah the foundations of Rome were laid by Romulus, the legends say; about the time that Cyrus proclaimed liberty to the Jews by the Euphrates the last of the "seven kings"—Tarquinius Superbus—began to reign by the Tiber; and when Ezra was sent to govern Judea Coriolanus was banished from Rome.

The stream of Roman history began to glow with new light when, in the days of the first Emperor Augustus, a greater than Augustus appeared as the "Babe of Bethlehem," before whom the race is yet to bow and "crown him Lord of all." Little did the men who made Rome the power and the terror it was dream that its aggressions and control were but preparations for the coming of One mightier than any or all of the rulers over the vast empire. Forerunners of the King of kings were all these crowned and sceptered chieftains. They built their ships that Paul and his associates might sail the Eastern seas. They stretched out broad and smooth and well-defended highways that God's word of gospel grace might the more swiftly run. Thus man's work furthers God's plan. They unify government and spread abroad a common speech, that Hebrew truth, informed by a new and living Spirit, may sweep from east to west, from north to south, and give news of one salvation to all men every-where.

Thereafter Rome occupies an important place in ecclesiastical history, from the days of Paul, the "Roman citizen," to these times, when Pope Leo XIII. sits in the Vatican as head of the Romish Church, while Protestant

Churches—European and American—proclaim a free gospel under the shadow of St. Peter's.

It would seem as if all manner of experiments were to be made in Rome. The saint in the Catacombs was to try the effect of persecution and affliction on Christian faith. Worldly prosperity, with king on the throne and the disciples of the lowly One in palaces, was to show the Church through succeeding ages how bad a thing for the followers of the Cross-bearer are wealth and honor, ease and luxury. Supreme ecclesiastical control for centuries, with pope in power and the crowns of kingdoms at his feet, were to demonstrate the peril of temporal power in hands that should be empty and outstretched in persuading the race to forsake all and to follow Christ.

Rome has her lessons for the true Church of Jesus Christ, lessons of warning, emphatic and earnest, against worldly ambition, greed of gold, and earthly influence.

A brighter day dawns for Rome and for the race. For a time indeed—since the end is not yet—might shall conquer right, the Pharisee scorn the penitent publican, and the chains bind bodies of those whom Christ has made free; but, lo! the triumph cometh. An open Bible, a free people, just laws, human pity and help, a full salvation, shall yet be found in Rome; the Rome of ancient and of modern oppressions, the Rome of the heroic Paul, the Rome of the faithful few to whom, in the early days of our faith, Paul wrote his words of

greeting, of doctrine, of exhortation, and of consolation.
And it is an interesting fact that while memories of
ancient prowess and of ancient culture, of mediæval
splendor, and of later heroism, give fascination to the
pages of Roman history, the name that is to-day most
alive, most suggestive and inspiring, is that of the
great apostle to the Gentiles, whose labors and writ-
ings are so intimately associated with the great city on
the Tiber.

JOHN H. VINCENT.

BUFFALO, N. Y., *April*, 1889.

CONTENTS.

CHAPTER VIII.

CHAPTER IX.

M A P S.

ANALYSIS.

First Period.

ROME UNDER THE KINGS. 753–509 B. C.—244 YEARS.

Second Period.

THE ROMAN REPUBLIC. 509–31 B. C.—478 YEARS.

I. Rise of Plebs, and Rise of Rome. 509–264 B. C.
II. Punic Wars and Foreign Conquests. 264–133 B. C.
III. Civil Wars and Fall of Republic. 133–31 B. C.

Third Period.

THE ROMAN EMPIRE. 31 B. C.–476 A. D.—507 YEARS.

I. From Augustus to Commodus. 31 B. C.–192 A. D.
II. The Decline and Fall. 192–476 A. D.

Conclusion.

TO THE FALL OF THE EASTERN EMPIRE. 1453 A. D.

Tacitus.

ITALY

Roman Military Roads ————
Fortresses, or Colonies - - - - -

OUTLINE HISTORY OF ROME.

CHAPTER I.

PRELIMINARY—ITALY AND THE ITALIANS—ROME
AND THE ROMANS.

A LONG, narrow peninsula swings out from the
body of Europe into the Mediterranean Sea, tending to the eastward as it falls. Its contour on the
map bears a singular and lively resemblance to a
human leg and foot. The central mountain range
suggests strength, and the tip of the toe poised
above the triangular island of Sicily suggests
vigorous action. That strong peninsular limb,
drawn back toward the east and ready to sweep
forward toward the west, may fitly represent the
Rome of history; restless, aggressive, mighty,
disturbing the waters of the Mediterranean and
sending heavy swells of war and conquest to
every shore that guards the sea, and many a
league beyond—to Parthia on the Caspian and to
Britain in the Atlantic.

The history which lies before us is not the
history of this boot-shaped Italian peninsula ; it is
the remarkable record of the rise and development of a single Italian city from a position of

insignificant weakness to the sovereignty, not only of Italy, but of the world. Grecian history centers now in Sparta, now in Thebes, now in Athens, now in Macedon ; but Roman history is the story of the acts and achievements of one city through twelve centuries of its growth, eminence, and decline. This single sovereign city was Rome.

The way to the study of Roman history lies through a knowledge of the geography of Italy; for it is to this peninsula that Roman influence and authority were confined during the first five centuries of the city's existence.

Italy is the central of the three peninsulas of southern Europe, Spain lying to the west, and the Balkan peninsula, with Greece at its extremity, on the east. The Alps mountains, massive and lofty, cut it off from the continent, the two piers of their arch resting on the gulfs of Genoa and Venice. On the east is the Adriatic, which the Romans called the Upper Sea, in distinction from the Lower, or Tuscan Sea, which washed their western shores. The Ionian Sea, on the south, rolls between "the sole of the boot" and Greece, completing the natural boundaries. The extreme length of Italy from Mount Blanc, in the northern highlands, to the southernmost point of Calabria, measures about seven hundred miles. From the tip of the heel in Calabria to the tip of the toe at Rhegium it is two hundred miles as the crow flies. The breadth of the northern expansion is a little over three hundred miles. The ordinary width of the peninsula is about one hundred miles. The area of the country is somewhat less than one hundred thousand square miles, and is about twice that of the State of New York.

The Alps and the Apennines are the only considerable mountain ranges. The former reach the height of fifteen thousand feet and present a difficult but not impassable barrier to foreign invasion. Where the Alps descend toward the sea at their south-western end the Apennines have their beginning. This long and somewhat open chain at first trails eastward to the Adriatic and then turns sharply to the south, keeping the middle of the peninsula for a few hundred miles as a rocky midrib, and in the far south breaking up into a net-work of hills with intervening valleys. Besides these two main ranges there are a few famous volcanic summits, some wildly active, others long at rest. These are Ætna, in Sicily, and Mount Vultur, the Alban Hills, and Vesuvius, on the mainland.

The Padus, or Po—Virgil's "King of Rivers"—is the one large river of Italy. With its tributaries—the Trebia, Ticinus, Addua, and Mincius—and the Athesis or Adige, it waters the great plain of Lombardy, as we call the flat district which lies between the Alps and the Apennines. The other streams are small, and flow from the central watershed, eastward or westward, to the sea. The Adriatic receives the Rubicon, Metaurus, Frento, and Aufidus ; the Macra, Arnus, Tiber, Liris, Vulturnus and Silarus flow into the Tuscan Sea.

Until late in the history of Rome the valley of the Po was not considered politically a part of Italy, the northern boundary of which was not the Alps, but the Apennine mountains and the water-courses Macra and Rubicon. This section, Northern, or Continental Italy, as it is variously called, differed widely from the southern portion, or Italy Proper, in physical features, population, and history. Northern Italy included three distinct regions: Liguria, on the west, skirting the Gulf of Genoa, Venetia, eastward, on the Gulf of Venice, and between them Gallia Cisalpina,* or Hither Gaul, abounding in fertile fields, populous cities, and brave men.

Among the towns of Northern Italy were Vercellæ, Augusta Taurinorum and Genoa, in Liguria; Patavium and Aquileja, in Venetia; and in Cisalpine Gaul, Mediolanum, Ticinum, Cremona, Mantua, Bononia, Placentia, Lucca, and Ravenna.

The country south of the Rubicon was Italy Proper of the Romans. It was made up of two general divisions, Central and Lower Italy.

Central Italy extended from the little rivers

---

* Gallia Cisalpina means Gaul this side the Alps, or Hither Gaul, as distinguished from Gallia Transalpina, or Farther Gaul, the modern France. Cisalpine Gaul, was likewise called Gallia Togata, because its people might wear the Roman robe or toga. The Transalpine Gauls were *braccati*— that is, "clad in breeches."

Macra and Rubicon, on the north, to the Silarus
and Frento, on the south, and from sea to sea.
The central mountain range and tribal differences
subdivided its territory into six districts.   On the
Tuscan sea-coast were Etruria, Latium and Campania, and beyond the highlands were Umbria,
Picenum, and Samnium.

Etruria lay in the well-watered plain which
was left by the Apennines as they bowed toward
the east.   Its inhabitants, the Etruscans, were
already an ancient race when Rome was founded.
They had made progress in civilization and the
arts, and their fleets were strong in the seas of the
west.   Lake Trasimenus was in their territory, as
were the towns Volaterræ, Arretium, Clusium,
Cære, and Veii, long a rival of Rome.   Just south
of Etruria, and almost midway of the peninsula,
lay Latium, a narrow strip of hill and plain between the Tiber and the Liris.   Here, in a league
of thirty communities, dwelt in very early times
the Latins.   Here, also, were the Æqui, Hernici,
and Volsci, of slightly different blood and language.
Prominent among the Latin towns were Alba
Longa, Tibur, Præneste, Minturnæ, Antium, Arpinum, Fregellæ, and pre-eminent among all the
towns of Latium, indeed, of all the world, Rome.

Still farther south was Campania, whose sunny
skies and fertile hill-sides early attracted the Grecian colonists, and in the later days of Roman
luxury filled it with the costly villas of senators
and knights.   Here was Cumæ, where the Sibyl

had guarded her magic books ; Baiæ, in whose
waters emperors delighted to bathe ; Capua, whose
pleasures made Hannibal forget his oath ; Mi•
senum, the head-quarters of the imperial fleet;
Neapolis, on its famous bay ; and near at hand
Herculaneum and Pompeii, under the threatening
brow of Vesuvius.

The district known as Umbria extended from the
Adriatic over the crown of the Apennines to the
borders of Etruria and Latium. The Tiber had
its sources among these Umbrian hills, and within
these borders were the towns of Ariminum, Spo-
letium, Narnia, and Sentinum. Picenum was a
land of peace and plenty lying along the adjacent
coast. Its people were of the Samnite stock, and
near them lived the related Marsi, Pæligni, and
Frentani. In the Picene territory were Ancona,
a Roman naval station, and Asculum, a fortress
whose reduction long taxed the strength of Rome.

The Samnites occupied a range of the interior
highlands and a seaboard strip on the Adriatic.
They were hardy and frugal, like the early Romans,
and retained these simple virtues and the military
spirit which sprang from them long after the
Roman type had lost its best characteristics. The
neighboring and kindred tribe of Sabines was one
of the first to come in contact with the rising city,
and the Samnites themselves were the most persistent enemies of Roman dominion in Italy.
Reate, Amiternum, and Cures were the best-known
towns of the Sabine land. And Rome had reason

to remember the names of the Samnite fortresses, Corfinium, Sulmo, Bovianum, Beneventum, and especially Caudium, the scene of a notable disaster.

Lower Italy embraced all the peninsula south of the Silarus and Frento rivers. Its districts were four: Apulia, Calabria, Lucania, and Bruttium. So many colonies from Greece had settled in the warm nooks of this lovely coast that the whole region received the name of Magna Grecia, or Great Greece. Apulia was a land of shepherds and herdsmen. Cannæ, on the Aufidus, was the most famous of its plains. Here, too, near the same river and below the silent crater of Mount Vultur, was Venusia, the birth-place of the poet Horace.

Calabria, the heel of Italy, had both grazing lands and farmsteads. Two of its towns are prominent in history: Tarentum, the Greek colony which vainly withstood the power of Rome, and Brundisium, the port of embarkation for travelers bound from Italy to the Orient.

The broad Tarentine Gulf rolled between Calabria and Bruttium, " the toe," and Lucania, "the instep" of Italy. In Lucania were numerous Greek towns—Pæstum, Metapontum, and Heraclea. Sybaris, whose luxury contributed the word " sybarite " to our vocabulary, was in Bruttium, as were Croton, Locri, and, at the very tip-toe, commanding the Sicilian straits, Rhegium.

At an early date there were no Italian islands, but the authority of Rome at length brought the

2

neighboring Sicily (Trinacria), Sardinia, and Corsica within the Italian domain, together with the
islets and groups Elba, Malta, Capri, Liparæ, and
Ægusæ. The three larger islands furnished a
share of the Roman breadstuffs, and Sicily, which
had been settled by both Greeks and Carthaginians
before the rise of Rome, had many thriving towns
—Messana on the straits, Catana at the foot of
Ætna, Agrigentum, Lilybæum, Drepanum, Panormus—names which will occur again in the narrative, and Syracuse, a royal capital for whose possession three empires made Sicily their battle-ground.

The extent of the peninsula from north to south,
and the large amount of high land included within
its boundaries, give to Italy a great diversity of
climate. Its northern boundary is on the parallel
of Quebec, in Canada, and the city of Richmond,
in Virginia, has the same latitude as its southern
extremity ; yet from several causes the differences
of heat and cold are less than this comparison
would suggest. For the mountains modify the
climate, and the surrounding seas temper and
moisten the winds which blow to Italy across
their surface. In consequence the plains of upper
Italy enjoy a temperate and generally healthful
climate. The Alps shut in the Po valley from the
hard winters of Central Europe; but chilling blasts
sometimes swoop down from their icy summits to
render summer days comfortless. The strip of
sea-coast between the Apennines and the Gulf of
Genoa—the modern Riviera—is a winter paradise.

Central Italy—the Italy of Rome and Latium —is in the latitude of Boston, but its winters are mild and the hot season is not intolerable. Little snow falls except in the highlands, and the rivers seldom freeze. From Campania southward the land enjoys almost perpetual summer. Magna Grecia is semi-tropical in its warmth and moisture, and Sicily has a well-earned reputation for unclouded skies. The frequent references of the Latin poets to nipping frosts, snow-capped hills, and ice-bound rivers have prompted the question whether the climate of ancient Italy was no more severe than that of the same districts in modern times; and it is now believed that the disappearance of the forests, which in the old times covered a large part of the peninsula, has affected both the temperature and the amount of rainfall. There have always been drawbacks from the pleasures of life in Italy. From the days of the foundation of Rome the lowlands of Latium and other regions have been haunted by malarial germs. The Roman Campagna was, and is, a plague-spot ; the marsh lands of Etruria and the stagnant lagoons of Venetia poison the air at certain seasons of the year, and at times the Sirocco, a burning wind from the African deserts, sweeps across the sea bringing fever and blight. But these were the only exceptions to the general beauty and comfort of the land. Italy was "sunny" then as now. The vine and olive have flourished and come to perfection on its hill-sides since the early days when the

Romans thought Saturn, the father of the gods, set them there. Besides the rich olive-oil and delicate wine the land yielded the ruder staples— wheat, flax, and hemp. Orchard and forest fruits were abundant and various. The large fruit of the chestnut-tree was an important feature of the yearly harvest, and lemons, oranges, figs, almonds, and dates were plentiful and cheap. Sections of the country were peculiarly adapted to the profitable raising of sheep and oxen, and agriculture or grazing was the natural industry of the Italian.

The clear and brilliant atmosphere gave to the Italian skies a richness of color which has always been the admiration of poets and the despair of painters. The omnipresent mountains and the never distant sea lend to the landscape a living and ever changing charm. The bays and inlets of the south, together with the tangle of the adjacent mountains, present a resemblance to the Grecian landscape which could not have been lost upon the impressionable colonists from Attica and the Peloponnesus who settled here. Elsewhere the resemblance to Greece is noticeably wanting. The shores are low and regular. The mountains seldom approach the coast, and their general form is such that they do not form partition walls to shut up cities to themselves, like the Greek cantons, where every rock-walled valley was a State. It has been often and truthfully said that Greece and Italy, though side by side, lie back to back ; for the life and movement of the former were directed east-

ward from Athens, Thebes, and Sparta by means
of the Ægean Islands—stepping-stones to the
hospitable shores of Asia. But on the side toward
Greece Italy had but two harbors, Ancona and
Brundisium. Rome, Genoa, and Naples faced the
setting sun, and the Roman armies had proved
their prowess against Sicily, Sardinia, and Carthage before the first Roman trireme crossed the
Ionian Sea to plant the Roman standard on Hellenic soil.

The first inhabitants of Italy of whom any thing
is known were the Iapygians, who entered the
peninsula from the north and retreated southward
before successive waves of immigration. A few in-
decipherable inscriptions in their language remain;
but in the Roman times they had ceased to be a
nation of any strength or influence, having lost
their individuality by blending it with the stronger
Greek race which colonized their territory and reduced them to subjection. The Italians who followed were of the same Aryan or Indo-European family as the Iapygians. The Aryans are
supposed to have lived before the dawn of history,
on one of the great table-lands of Central Asia.
Thence from time to time, as their limits became
too narrow for their necessities, colonies set out ;
not a few persons to found a town, but men,
women, and children by the million to find homes
and plant nations. These successive throbs of immigration were doubtless centuries apart, and
these floods of people deluged both India and

Europe. There is no record of these migrations.
They took place before the days of writing, and
no intelligible tradition has come down from those
misty days. But the scientific comparison of the
ancient languages has enabled scholars to group
these nations in families and to calculate the bond
of relationship between them. Thus it has been
proved that the Italians were closely related to the
Hellenes or Greeks; that in their westward journeyings from the first home in Asia the two nations were in company long enough to acquire
many common traits of character, to practice similar customs, and in some cases to employ the same
words to express their thoughts. The probable
route of this hypothetical migration lay through
Asia Minor, across the Bosphorus, and through
Thrace. Here the Hellenes turned southward to
occupy their peninsula and to give it renown, while
their former fellow-travelers moved on slowly
toward the north-west, doubling the head of the
Adriatic in the lapse of centuries and pouring
down into the fertile prairie-lands of the Po. The
ages which had intervened since their separation
from the Greeks had wrought changes in the Italian character and language, and it was a stern,
hardy, and unimaginative race that peopled Italy,
pushing the gentle Iapygians before them.

There were marked differences among the Italians themselves. Slight but essential variations
in their use of the common language show plainly
that the stock was divided. · One part, composed

of the Umbrians and Samnites, and hence called
the Umbro-Sabellian branch (including also Sabines and Oscans), found its home among the
mountains of Central and Southern Italy, and
spread thence to the Adriatic coast. The other
branch, the Latins, dwelt in the hill-encircled plain
on the east side of the peninsula south of the
Tiber. It was, perhaps, less numerous than its
congener of the adjacent highlands, but it was
more fortunate in its location. For within its territory and of its people were the Romans, who
raised the Latin name and tongue to the first rank
in Italy.

Besides the retiring Iapygians and the conquering Italians, a third important race, the Etruscan,
had its home in Italy, coming whence and when
is scarcely known. These people were probably
Aryans, like their neighbors, but differently developed and leaving Asia at another era. Their
resemblance to the Greeks and Italians was remote
and indistinct. The accepted theory is that they
came into the peninsula by the land route and
settled in the Po valley until expelled by stronger
invaders. They then crossed the Apennines and
made their home in the district north of Latium,
between the Tiber and Arnus, which is still called
Tuscany in honor of their name. Here in early
times they had a league of twelve strong communities, and it was their strength and superior civilization which placed the first serious check upon
the power of Rome. Etruria attained its prime

about five centuries before Christ. It was then a
naval power, and its fleets met those of Greece
and Carthage in equal combat. But the following
century saw its decline, and by rapid degrees its
territory and authority were acquired by Rome.

In the earliest historic times two other nations
appeared in Italy—the Gauls or Celts in the north,
and the Greeks in the south. These Celts were
an off-shoot of the Germanic stock, which spread
over western Europe and founded Germany,
France, Spain, and Britain. The Gauls took full
possession of the Po valley and gained for it the
name of Cisalpine Gaul. Though barbarians by
race they early adopted civilization, and in the
time of Cæsar they were admitted to the full dig-
nities of Roman citizenship.

Unlike the four first-named peoples, Iapygians,
Italians, Etruscans and Celts, who entered Italy
through the Alpine passes on the north, the Greeks
came in at the south and by sea. Again unlike
the others, they were not a migrating nation, but
a succession of colonies sent out to relieve the
overflowing cities of Greece. The time of their
earliest settlements is in the vicinity of 1000 B. C.,
when the close of the Trojan War sent many a
crew of mariners in quest of new adventures.
The process of colonization extended through
four centuries, and Greek cities sprang up thickly
along the southern and western coasts as far north
as Cumæ and the Bay of Naples. Temples, theaters, and schools arose wherever the Greeks found

an abiding-place, and the wealth and extravagant luxury of Magna Grecia were proverbial before the name of Rome was known beyond its narrow circle of Latin towns.   But the Greek cities, with the fatal political weakness of their race, preferred individual independence to union against a common enemy; and so it happened that, when the strug-

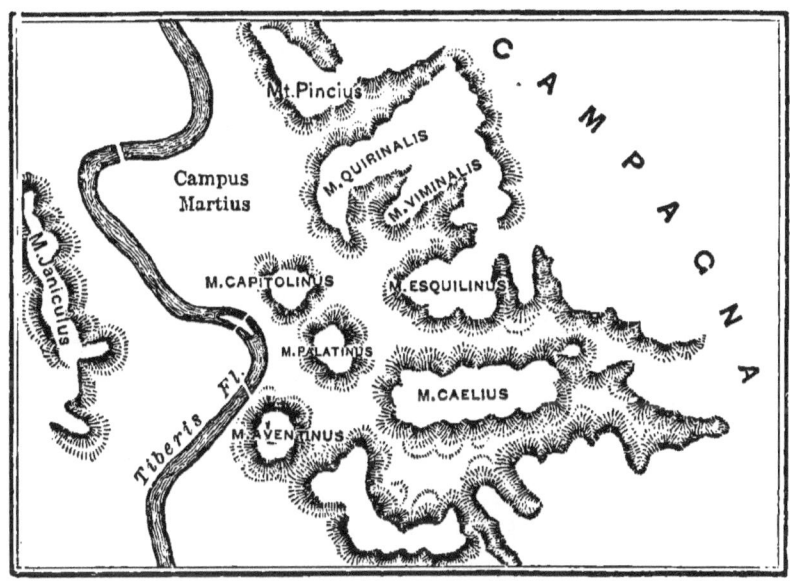

THE SITE OF ROME.

gle for supremacy came, the baths and theaters of these elegant towns availed them nothing against the rude strength of the Roman commonwealth.

What, then, was Rome, and what manner of men were the Romans that, one after the other, the several races of the peninsula bowed at her bidding? The remainder of this volume will be an answer to this inquiry.   But the answer will be clearer if the

student will bear in mind the physical features of
"the Eternal City" and the characteristics of the
Romans themselves.

The city was built on a cluster of low hills
in Latium, on the left bank of the river Tiber,
a few miles below its junction with the Anio,
and twenty-two miles from its mouth at Ostia,
on the Tuscan Sea. As it approaches the site of
Rome the Tiber turns sharply toward the east, and
then as sharply doubles back toward the west, thus
forming a rude S. In the upper loop of the S is a
broad plain on which the modern city, the capital
of Italy, is mainly built; but in the early times this
was the parade-ground of the army, the muster-
field of the populace, and was called the Campus
Martius (Field of Mars), from the Roman god
of war. Opposite the lower bend of the river are
the hills of the ancient city. Almost on the bank
are the Capitoline, Palatine, and Aventine, and
farther away, separated from these as by the hollow
or palm of a mighty hand, rise four finger-like eminences, the Cælian, Esquline, Viminal and Quirinal.
The sacred Capitoline bore the Arx, or citadel, and
the splendid temple of Jupiter. Up the slope of
this hill moved the famous processions of victorious
generals, and from the precipitous Tarpeian Rock
on its water-side criminals were hurled to destruction. At the base of the hill was the Tullianum,
a dungeon in which, among other noted prisoners,
St. Peter is said to have been confined. On the
adjoining Palatine Hill were the colossal buildings

which served the Emperors Augustus and Nero
for a residence, and which have given the name
palace (*palatium*) to any house fit for a king. Between this pile of palaces and the Aventine—the
people's hill—was the Circus Maximus, where
200,000 persons might witness the sword-fights,
races, and rough sports which constituted the
Roman games. The low ground between these
three hills and the river-bank was drained by an
ancient sewer, the Cloaca Maxima, and was assigned to the produce and cattle markets. The
principal market and meeting-place of the city,
however, was the Roman Forum, which was situ-
ated at the base of the Capitoline Hill, in the hollow
of the great Roman hand. The Forum was, in fact,
an open public square about 750 feet long by 250
broad. As a market-place of the little city it
naturally became the scene of public assembly for
many important purposes. A space near one end,
raised and cut off from the rest, was the Comitium or
official assembly-room of the citizens, and between
this and the Forum proper was the rostrum, or
speaker's stand, from which the magistrates addressed the citizens or the populace. On one or
two sides the Forum was lined with shops, but on
the south was a row of law-courts and temples,
among which the shrine of the goddess Vesta was
the most notable. Past these temples ran the Via
Sacra (Sacred Street), by which the triumphal
processions approached the Capitol. On the opposite of the square was the Curia, or Senate

Chamber. The world centered in Rome, and Rome centered in the Forum, where, in the time of the empire, stood a golden milestone, toward which all roads led and from which all distances in the realm were measured.

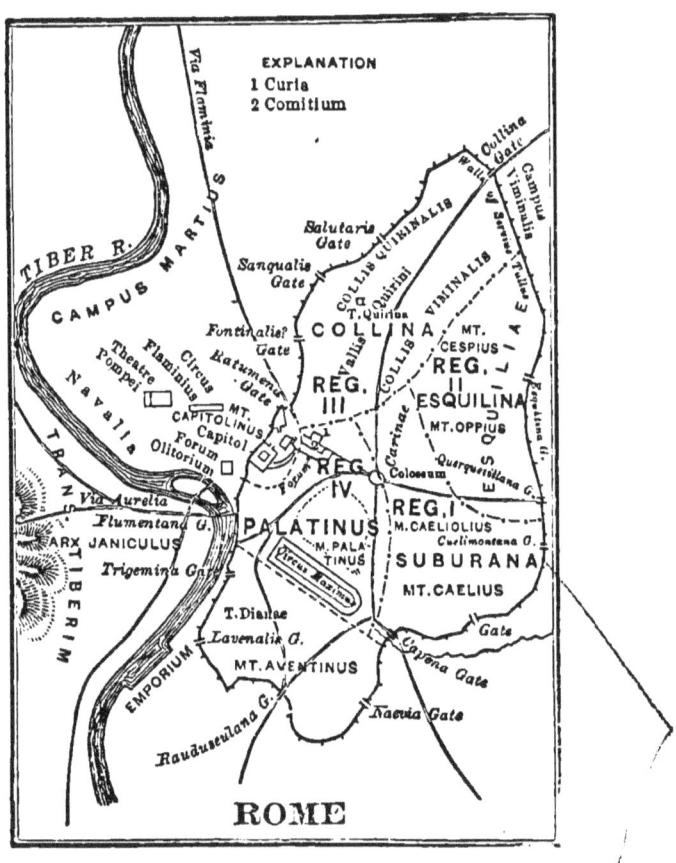

In this same hollow of the hills was the Suburra, the meanest and most crowded quarter of the city, and on its border, in bitter proximity, was the Carinæ, the dwelling-place of the richest and proudest

of the citizens. In the adjacent lowlands, but nearer
the slope of the Esquiline, still stands the ruined
Colosseum, the remains of the Flavian Amphitheater, within whose arches 80,000 cruel Romans
have looked on while Christian women were
"butchered to make a Roman holiday." The four
outer hills seem to have been less thickly settled
than the others ; but in the period of the city's
splendor they, too, were covered with magnificent
baths and public parks and gardens. Two hills,
not to be included in the famous seven, were situ-
ated on the right bank of the Tiber. These are the
Vatican, now occupied as the papal residence, and
the Janiculus, a Roman fortress. Modern Rome
has a population of 300,000. In the reign of the
Emperor Augustus it had 2,000,000 inhabitants.

How did Rome become so populous and powerful ? The answer to this question does not appear
at first sight. The geographical situation possessed
no pre-eminent advantages, such as set apart Constantinople, Alexandria, London, and New York
for centers of trade and population. The harbors
of Italy are at Venice, Naples, Leghorn, Genoa,
not on the bank of the Tiber; and Rome was the
natural market-place of Latium only, by no means
the largest or most fertile division of the peninsula.
It cannot be doubted, therefore, that the wealth and
commercial rank of Rome were the consequences,
and not the causes, of the city's political supremacy.
The elements of Rome's political strength are to
be sought in the character of her people.

During the long period covered by " the making
of Rome " the Romans had six distinguishing national traits: they were unpolished, superstitious,
proud, stern, and steadfast, and possessed a real
genius for law and government.

Rudeness and simplicity marked their manners
and customs. Agriculture, war, politics, and but
little else, concerned the citizens. In refinement
of thought and action, in art and literature, they
were the imitators of the Greeks, whose effeminacy
they affected to despise, but whose graces they
assiduously copied. Their national games were
coarse and brutal. Chariot races, combats of men
with wild beasts and with each other, were to the
Roman what the competitions in athletics and
in poetry and rhetoric were to the Greek. The
foreign conquests, which at length filled the city
with public and private plunder, put an end to this
age of simplicity. The frugality and the steady
habits of the early Roman gave place to lavish extravagance and gross dissipation, which
had a potent influence in the city's ultimate ruin.

Roman superstition is shown in the religion of
the State. Not until they had dipped into the
fanciful mythology of the Greeks did the Romans
think of their gods as possessing human form and
being subject to human passions. The divinities
were many, and represented phases of nature as
well as the interests of the household and the nation. Jupiter was the sky, and ruled over all gods
and men. Juno was the guardian of motherhood.

Minerva was wise, Mars warlike, and Vesta the patron of the State. Besides Ceres, Saturn, Mercury, Neptune, and others of almost equal rank, there were lesser divinities to attend to the varied activities of business and domestic life, and in every Roman household the *lares* and *penates* were the objects of daily supplication. In the Roman mind religion was a contract, and worship was the human share in the bargain. The worshiper gave vows, prayers, festivals, and fasts, and in return demanded as his right the favor of the gods. The State took charge of the religion, and supported a complex system of priests and wise men to superintend the religious observances. Of the former class were the Flamens, who officiated in the temples, and the Vestal Virgins, who kept the eternal fire on the altar of the State in the shrine of Vesta. Of the wise men were the Augurs, the Pontifices, Fetiales, etc. The Augurs consulted the will of the gods by observing the actions of certain sacred birds, the Pontifices interpreted the omens which the Augurs observed, and thus had great political power, since, by declaring the gods unpropitious, a public assembly might be dissolved, an election postponed, or the passage of an obnoxious law prevented. The Pontifex Maximus, or "pope," was the head of the State religion. The Fetiales were the envoys or heralds of the State; they protected the sanctity of treaties and were the agents of the Senate in fixing boundaries and in declaring war. The Haruspices, like the Augurs, consulted the gods, but in a stranger fashion. It was their duty to seek for omens in the entrails of the sheep and oxen slaughtered for the sacrifices. This religion, with its gloomy rites and with its superstitious faith in omens, sufficed for the days of unreasoning faith, but it had completely lost its hold upon the thinking classes before the advent of Christianity.

The pride of a Roman noble or patrician was colossal. The internal history of the State through the first four centuries revolves about the resistance of a few patrician families to any encroachment upon their privileges and honors. The commons or plebeians were not legally citizens, and it was the fixed policy of the patricians that they should not be. No plebeian might hold office, and the intermarriage of the two orders brought disgrace and social degradation to the patrician, whether man or woman. At last the barrier fell, and the class pride gave way to the common pride in citizenship, which the consolidated Romans guarded as jealously from the Italians and provincials as the patricians had fortified it against the plebs.

To his rude manners, his superstitious mind, and his haughty demeanor the Romans added a sternness of spirit which at times deserves no better name than cruelty. Their history abounds in anecdotes of magistrates who sentence their sons to death, of generals who devote themselves to death to save their armies, of noble youths who throw away their lives to propitiate the offended gods, or who hold their right hands in the flames to prove to an alien king that torture has no terrors for a Roman. " Callousness to human suffering was a Roman virtue," and the pages of history are red with Roman slaughterings.

" As faithful as a Roman sentinel " is the world's highest tribute to fidelity, and, in truth, the Pompeian soldier who was pelted to death at his post by the fiery hail of Vesuvius grandly typifies the steadfastness of the Roman character. It may have been the outcome of the stern discipline which the father in the family, the consul in the city, and the general in the army consistently enforced, or it may have been an inborn virtue; but this splendid trait stands out in every relation of their common life and at every turn of their history. In politics, under the name of "conservatism," it was this faculty of standing by settled principles which made the Roman constitution so slow in its development and so stable in its strength; and in war it was this same firmness of purpose which enabled the single city to maintain itself against Greek, Celtic, and Carthaginian invasions, and, without the aid of conspicuous generals or remarkable statesmen, to drive the invaders out of Italy, pursue them to their homes, and vanquish them.

Couple with the pertinacity of the Romans their exquisite political faculty and seek no farther for the sources of the Roman power. This faculty is

3

expressed in their respect for law and their correct understanding and application of the principles of justice ; it is pre-eminently exhibited in
the skill with which they adapted the constitution
to the changing conditions imposed by the extension of the Roman realm. These changes did not
take place in popular convulsions, rending the State,
but came through long periods of agitation, and
finally as the result of compromise.

From this description of the land and the people we pass on to their history.

CHAPTER II.

FIRST PERIOD.

ROME UNDER THE KINGS. (244 YEARS.) 753–509 B. C.

WHOEVER attempts to trace the history of an ancient State must come to a point in the remote past of which there are no written records. Yet the student of Roman history finds a detailed account of what are professedly the acts of the people of the ancient city from the very day of its foundation. The record which confronts us is one which the Romans themselves made and believed. Their later historians used it with little doubt of its authenticity. Their poets went to it for material with which to adorn their patriotic verse. Even the European scholars seem to have accepted its statements as substantial truth until a little more than a century ago. The doubts which were then first quietly suggested were put forward in more positive form by the German historian, Niebuhr (1776–1831), who proved, to the satisfaction of himself and many others, that the common account of the early Rome was rather poetry than history, and rested only upon a slight basis of truth. More recent investigation has modified Niebuhr's

conclusions, and the substance of modern belief is
this : That the history of Rome previous to the
fourth century before Christ is a fabric in which
certain main outlines are true, while the masses
of detail which make up the narrative are either
greatly exaggerated or entirely imaginary. The
argument for the rejection of the greater part of
the story as it stands is unanswerable. It is rich
in incredible marvels and miracles, its chronology
is involved and inconsistent, and it relates as facts
certain undoubted fables borrowed from the legends of other Aryan nations. Yet the ground-
work of truth which underlies this quicksand of
invention forbids the historian to disregard it.
The legends will be given here at such length as
the limits of the volume permit, and with the understanding that they are not offered as genuine
history. The fanciful narrative will be followed
by the true story in the shape in which modern
scholars believe it.

The legends ran in this wise :

After the Greeks had taken the city of Troy, in
Asia Minor, Æneas, the son of Priam, the Trojan
king, escaped, with many companions, and came
by sea to the western coast of Italy, where he
founded Lavinium, on the shore of Latium. For
three hundred years the Trojan line ruled the
Latin tribes, having their royal seat at Alba
Longa, the " long white " city on the Alban Mount.
In time two sons, Numitor and Amulius, were
born to Silvius Procas, king of the Albans. The

latter usurped his brother's throne and consecrated his brother's daughter, Rhea Silvia, a vestal virgin, in order to extirpate the line of Numitor. But when, by the war god Mars, the vestal became the mother of twin sons, their cruel uncle had the babes thrown into the Tiber. The river was swollen with the spring floods and the boys floated ashore unharmed, and lodged in the branches of a fig-tree on the inundated meadow at the foot of a hill called Palatinus. A she-wolf took pity on them and nourished them with her whelps. In these strange surroundings the twins were discovered by a shepherd of those regions, who adopted

Romulus.

them out of pity. The boys were named Romulus and Remus, and lived among the herdsmen until they reached manhood, when they learned of their origin, killed their wicked uncle, and re-established their grandfather, Numitor, on the throne of the Albans. But the young princes had ambitions of their own, and, soon collecting a little colony, they founded a new city on the Palatine hill which Romulus, favored by the gods, called from his own name Rome. April 21, 753 B. C., was the accepted date of this momentous act. The slighted Remus showed his derision of the puny defenses of his brother's city by leaping over its walls ; whereat Romulus, in his anger, slew him, declaring that a similar fate

awaited all future assailants of the city. On the
neighboring Capitoline Hill Romulus opened an
"asylum" or refuge for the oppressed and discon-
tented people of the surrounding country ; and as
wives were wanting for the new settlers the Sabines of the neighboring town of Cures were bid-
den to a religious festival at Rome ; the Roman
brigands seized the Sabine women while the
husbands and brothers were witnessing the games.
In the war which followed a Roman girl, Tarpeia,
betrayed the city in return for "what the Sabine
soldiers wore on their arms." But when she had
let the Sabines inside the capitol they crushed the
traitress with their heavy shields ; for these also
did they wear on their arms as well as the heavy
bangles of gold which had tempted the maiden.
Thanks to the intervention of the Sabine women,
this war ended in the union of the two tribes, and
until his death the Sabine chief reigned jointly
with the Roman. After this Romulus framed a
constitution for the State. A number of families
were set apart to be the "patricians," or nobles, to
distinguish them from the "plebeians," or commons,
who, though dwelling in the city, had no political power. The patricians were divided into three
tribes—Ramnes, Tities, and Luceres—each tribe being composed of ten wards or *curiæ*. From the
wisest patricians one hundred were chosen to form
an advisatory council, or senate, to assist the king
when called upon for their opinion, and from the
younger nobles was levied the first legion—an army

of 3,000 foot and 300 horse. When the new constitution had been put in working order the gods caught up Romulus from the sight of the people, but his name was revered, and he was worshiped as a divinity ever afterward under the name of Quirinus, on the Quirinal Hill.

For a year the throne was vacant before the Senate selected a worthy successor to the founder of the city. The choice fell upon a Sabine named Numa Pompilius, whose wife, the nymph Egeria, aided him much in his work of teaching the people the principles of morals and religion. He erected a temple to Vesta, the goddess of the home, and trained his subjects to be peaceful and pious. During the forty-three years of his reign the city was prosperous and happy.

Numa Pompilius.

Tullius Hostilius, the third king, was a great warrior. It was in his time that Rome began her conquests. The first struggle was with the mother-city, Alba Longa. In this war three Roman and three Alban brothers, the Horatii and the Curiatii, fought as champions for their respective armies, and by stratagem the Romans won after two of the Horatii had already fallen. In the end Alba was taken and burned, Rome succeeding to the older city's commanding place among the Latin towns. The warrior-king was rendered impious by his victories, and, although he fought stoutly for Rome against both the Etruscans and the Sabines, the offended gods destroyed him by a thunderbolt in the thirty-third year of his reign.

The fourth monarch in the line was Ancus Martius, the descendant and disciple of the holy Numa. He was both brave and good. Under him the gods were reverenced and the boundaries of the city were enlarged. He extended its authority still farther among the Latin towns, and fortified the Janiculan Hill on the right bank of the Tiber as a stronghold against Etruscan attack. The houses of the city spread over the Aventine, now that his victories brought so many new residents to Rome, and to its mouth the Tiber became a Roman river.

Of the first four rulers of the city two had been of Roman, two of Sabine blood. The fifth king was Etruscan. Lucumo, a man whose Greek father had migrated from Corinth to the Etruscan town of Tarquinii, removed to Rome in the days of Ancus Martius with Tanaquil, his able wife. Prophetic intimations of coming glory were not wanting, and, Romanizing his foreign name to Lucius Tarquinius, the new-comer took hold of public affairs with an energy and wisdom which won the approval of the king. Ancus made the foreigner the guardian of his young sons, and at their father's death the Senate preferred the guardian to his wards and put the scepter in the hands of Lucius Tarquinius, commonly called Tarquinius Priscus, or "Tarquin the Ancient." He was a worthy follower of Ancus. His prowess in battle overcame the Etruscans, who sent to him the golden crown, the scepter, the purple robe, the ivory chair, and the *fasces*, which remained forever the emblems of Roman authority. To conform the old constitution to the needs of the new metropolis the king doubled the number of senators and of the patrician tribes, and to make the city worthy of its rank he established annual games in the Circus Maximus, set apart the Forum for a public market and meeting-place, built the massive stone sewer, the Cloaca Maxima, which still drains the low ground between the hills, and commenced the erection of a temple of Jupiter on the Capitoline. Here the workmen dug up a human skull (*caput*), which was interpreted to mean that this spot was to be the capital of the world. Some of the ancient shrines were torn down to clear a space for the new temple; but the gods of youth and of boundaries resisted all attempts to remove them, and their chapels were left undisturbed, in token that the city should continually renew its vigorous youth and its boundaries should remain inviolate.

Tarquinius was an able ruler, but the sons of Ancus could not forget that his influence with the Senate had cost them the throne to which they had a fancied claim. Moreover, as the king waxed old

they perceived that Servius Tullius, the son of a
slave-girl of the palace, had found favor in his
sight. In their jealous rage they had the aged
king assassinated ; but before they could profit by
their crime Tanaquil, the sagacious queen, had
thwarted their plans. She addressed the people
from the palace-steps, telling them that her husband had been attacked and dangerously wounded,
and that Servius Tullius had the royal warrant to
conduct the business of the kingdom until the
monarch's recovery. Although coming to the
throne in this irregular manner Servius gradually
won to himself the support of both citizens and
Senate. He was a statesman-like ruler, and, apart
from his campaigns against the Etruscans, his
labors were those of peace. In his time a wall was
built inclosing the seven famous hills. But it is as
a political reformer that this king is best remembered. His lowly birth seems to have given him
sympathy with the plebeians, for it was by his
constitution that they were first admitted to any
share, however slight, in the government or defense of the city. Servius abolished the three
patrician tribes and re-divided all the people into
four tribes. Furthermore, and far more memorable, was his organization of the people into
classes and centuries for military and political
purposes. Admission to these classes depended
upon the amount of property which an individual
possessed, and was entirely independent of blood
nobility. The wealthiest young men were chosen

for cavalry duty, and were called equites (horsemen or knights). When the people were called together to vote upon any public matter, such as a dec-
laration of war, they assembled in accordance with
this military order, and their gathering was called
the *Comitia Centuriata*, the Assembly of the Centuries. This assembly, existing side by side with
the Senate, was for many hundred years the popular branch of the Roman legislature.

Tarquin the Ancient had left two sons, the gentle Aruns and the haughty Lucius. To these men
King Servius married the two Tullias, his daugh-
ters, who were as diversely tempered as their husbands. The match-making was wretchedly done,
and eventually Lucius put to death his wife and
brother and wedded his sister-in-law, a woman
after his own heart. The pair then compassed the
death of the good king, and it is said that Tullia,
hastening to greet her husband with his new title,
drove her chariot over the corpse of her gray-
haired father as it lay in the public street.

Lucius was the second of the Tarquins and the
last of the kings. Superbus, "the Haughty,"
was the name he bore, and merited. For he
walked not in the righteous statutes of his predecessor, but disregarded equally the old laws, the
advice of the Senate, and the reformed constitution. He enjoyed absolute sway, like the tyrants
who were in power in Greece at the same period,
and by his wars he placed Rome indisputably at
the head of the league of Latin towns. With the

spoils of his victories the city was adorned and the magic books of the Cumæan sybil were purchased. The king's successes hardened him in his iniquity, and the story runs that in his old age he sent his two sons and a nephew, Brutus, to Delphi in Greece to consult the oracle of Apollo, which had its temple there. Brutus was considered dull, but he secretly made a rich gift to the priestess and

rightly interpreted her response to the question which the envoys put to the oracle regarding the next ruler of the city. "He shall rule who first shall kiss his mother," was the simple answer, and while the two Tarquins were hastening homeward and drawing lots for the privilege the dull Brutus stumbled and pressed his lips to the earth, the mother of all things.

Lucius Junius Brutus.

Afterward the king's wild son, Sextus Tarquin, dishonored Lucretia, the wife of his cousin. Then the injured husband, with Brutus and other patriots, aroused the people to rid themselves of the tyrant and his family. So the Romans shut the gates against the monarch and swore a solemn oath to have no more kings, but in their stead to elect each year two consuls, or colleagues, of equal authority, to rule in war and peace. A long war followed. The Tarquins hatched conspiracies within the walls and instigated foreign invasions. Brutus, whom the citizens had made one of the first consuls, adjudged his own son to death for complicity in one of these plots. The people now banished the Tarquin family, root and branch, and took their corn-land, the Campus Martius, for a muster-field for the troops. Next the exiles sought Etruscan support, and the two cities, Tarquinii and Veii, aided them. Brutus fell in the great battle which the Romans fought near the wood of Arsia. Lars Porsena, the Etruscan king of Clusium, then befriended the Tarquins. He marched on Rome with an army, drove the defenders within the walls, and would have captured the city had not Horatius Cocles, with two more to help him, held the foe in play while the wooden bridge, which furnished the only approach to the city, was destroyed. Still Porsena besieged the city. Mucius Scævola, a Roman youth, failed in an attempt to kill the king in his tent. Scævola was seized and condemned to torture ; but to show his contempt of the sentence he thrust his right arm into the flame of an altar and held it steadily there until the hand was burned off. The king marveled at this exhibition of firmness and pardoned the boy. Then there was peace with the Romans, and the Tarquins had to turn from Porsena to the Latin towns for succor. The final contest was so desperate that the Romans dared not risk the divided leadership of two consular generals. In the place

of the two magistrates they appointed a single
commander-in-chief, or dictator, who had all the
power of the old kings, but who held office for
only six months at the longest. The first dictator,
Marcus Valerius Publicola, fell in with the Latins
near the shore of Lake Regillus, and beat them in
a bloody battle, the good gods, Castor and Pollux,
coming to lead the Roman legions just at the
critical moment when their ranks had begun to
waver before the mad charge of the last of the
Tarquins. This ended the struggle of the exiled
dynasty. The royal outlaw died at Cumæ, and for
five hundred years there was no king in Rome.

So ends the legendary story of the kings.

The historian has but a prosy substitute to offer
for the interesting fables which were so long accepted as the veritable annals of these early times.
And it must be remembered, furthermore, that he
is guided by no explicit records, and must state
probabilities where the wished-for facts are wanting. Overboard, then, with the cherished stories
of Trojan Æneas, of Romulus and Remus, and of
the seven kings, and clear the decks for action.

Reference has already been made to the Italian
race as the main division of the inhabitants of the
peninsula, and it has been related that the western
branch of this stock—the Latins—coming earlier
or with greater power, took for their abode the
hill-studded plain surrounded by the Tiber river,
the Apennine mountains, and the Volscian hills,
which here jut out along the Tuscan sea. It may

have been a thousand years before Christ that this
occupation took place, perhaps at the same time
that Solomon was ruling at Jerusalem and Homer
composing his Iliad in the Greek cities of Asia
Minor. These Latins were of a clannish spirit,
and agriculture was their only occupation. Thus
the descendants of a common ancestor lived together as a clan, and several clans tilling adjacent
tracts combined for mutual advantage in a larger
political body, or canton. Such a cantonal community would center about a village in some spot
easily capable of defense. To this citadel, for
which a hill would furnish the most eligible site,
the settlers would retire for safety in case of
danger. There were hostile tribes in the immediate neighborhood, not only the dreaded Etruscans, but rough Sabines and Samnites from the
mountain districts, and nearer yet the Æqui,
Hernici and Volsci. The common peril perhaps—
even more probably a community of race, to which
both language and religion bore witness—led the
Latin cantons to form a league. Good evidence
points to such a league of thirty members, the
head of which was Alba Longa, itself a canton-
center on the Alban mount, and probably the earliest Latin settlement in Latium. Here the Latins
celebrated the annual festival of their race.

One member of this league was Rome, the center
of its own canton. When and by whom the city
was really founded is now unknown. Strong
probability there is that three independent com-

munities had their citadels on as many of the
original hills of the city—the earliest on the
Palatine, the others on the Capitoline and Quirinal
—and that with characteristic political sagacity
the people of the three hill-communities combined to form a single stronger city-state, called
Rome, in which the original parts preserved their
identity for many generations in the three tribes
of Roman citizens—Ramnes, Tities and Luceres.
There is some evidence to show that at least one
of these uniting cantons was of Sabine race, thus
accounting for the legends of a Sabine union in
the reign of Romulus. This triple city, which by
its later expansion added four other eminences to
the original three, had now an advantage over the
surrounding towns. Three hills were better than
one ; a town on the river had more resources than
a rural village ; a frontier post must be jealously
defended, and a rude people could reap only gain
from frequent contact with a more polished nation.
So the Romans on the Tiber diversified their in-
dustries, adding trade with the river region to the
staple Latin occupation of farming and sheep-
raising. The other Latins could not object if
Rome fortified herself stoutly against the Etruscans, who were the foes of all ; and from her constant intercourse with these civilized foreigners
the Romans grew in grace and in knowledge of the
arts of war and peace. Thus we may believe that
Rome became a border fortress and agricultural
center, with some claim to commercial importance.

But it would be a mistake to suppose that Rome was rich and powerful in the times of the kings. Her wars were waged and her victories were gained with isolated towns, and the name of the city was hardly known outside the little circle of the league. Indeed, it is scarcely probable that her entire possessions at the time of the expulsion of the kings—about five centuries before Christ—comprised more than a strip of territory a few miles in width extending from the city to the sea along the left bank of the Tiber. Her influence, however, was somewhat wider than her boundaries, for by this time (509 B. C.) Alba Longa had been destroyed and her place in the Latin league usurped by Rome. The Latin towns retained their independence and Rome was not in any sense their ruler, except of a few which she had taken in war; but hers was now the weighty voice in the general councils of the league, and she presided at the national festival. At the close of this period, therefore, Rome had not yet achieved the mastery even of her nearest neighbors, although she had taken the first steps in that direction.

The government of Rome in the regal period is worthy of careful attention. Not all those who dwelt in the city were its legal citizens. The free population was composed of two distinct classes or orders : patricians and plebeians. The patrician order monopolized all political power and privilege. All offices of the State, all military commands (indeed, all military service), all priestly and pontifi-

4

cal positions, and all participation in the debates
or voting of the public assemblies was restricted to
these favored beings. The patricians ("children
of the fathers" the name implies) were probably
descended from the first settlers of these hills, and
it was to them alone that the triple tribal classifi-
cation into Ramnes, Tities, and Luceres applies.
These three patrician tribes or communities were
organized by families or households, ten families
making up one clan or *gens*, ten clans one ward or
curia, ten wards one community or *tribus*, although
this decimal division was not strictly carried out.
These three tribes formed the whole political body.
In theory they were the only citizens, and it was
of them alone that the term *populus*, "people,"
was rightly used.

At the outset the patricians (and their slaves)
were probably the only inhabitants, as well as
the only citizens, of Rome; but as the city grew in
power new residents were attracted. Latins were
brought to Rome from conquered towns; other
Latins were attracted to Rome for safety or for
the commercial facilities which began to exist there;
and these men and their descendants made up the
second Roman order, the plebeians—the word meaning the masses, the multitude, or the commons.
Some plebeians were directly dependent upon the
great patrician families, receiving support from
them and making return in service—a condition
not considered degrading, and certainly very far
from slavery. These were called *clients*, and their

patrician lords were their *patrons*. But by far the more numerous class were dependent upon no particular patrician. They enjoyed the protection of the whole citizen body and were free from any serious burdens of service or of taxation. They seem to have had large liberties in the city. They might buy and sell, and, if they could, get gain; they and their property were defended by the walls which the patricians had built, and their homes were guarded by the armies of the State, in which only patricians might serve. But politically they were not reckoned in the account at all. They were barred by law and custom from public career of any kind; there was no place which a plebeian might hold in the government, the army, or the Church, and he had not even the right to vote at the election of his patrician ruler. There was a great gulf fixed between the two orders which no man might pass. Wealth furnished no means of bridging the chasm. Birth alone, or the interposing favor of the king, determined his order. The intermarriage of the orders was illegal, and dragged the high-born party (man or woman) to the level of the plebeian. The absence of political rights was, in itself, hard enough to bear, but the arrogance and insolence of the aristocrats rendered intolerable the lot of a high-spirited commoner. It is important to understand the position of these two orders, for the internal history of the city for many years turns upon the patrician resistance to the plebeian demand for admission to political and social equality.

Apart from, and far beneath both orders, stood the Roman slaves. Slavery existed in the city in very early times, and its victims continued to increase in numbers throughout the city's history. The supply was drawn from all countries. Prisoners of war were naturally enslaved, and as Rome needed more servants than her conquests yielded she purchased them in the slave-markets of the East. Negro slaves were comparatively rare, but rough Gauls and Thracians herded with polished Greeks and Asiatics in the Roman slave-pens, and Syrians were chained with Egyptians at the oars of Roman triremes, and with them cultivated the soil of Campanian plantations. The slave-owner had power of life and death over his chattels, and oftentimes the condition of the Roman slave was horrible in the extreme, although a clement master would spare his human property.

The legends doubtless say truly that the earliest government was a monarchy, varying somewhat in its character in the two or three centuries of its existence and coming to a close in the curious aristocratic republic known as the Roman Commonwealth. The organization of the patrician order and its exclusive political powers have already been noticed, and it is now time to inquire how this power was exercised. In the first place, the whole citizen-body (namely, the patricians), which was the source of authority in the State, held meetings from time to time called the *Comitia Curiata*, or Assembly of the Curies. Theoretically this assem-

bly had high powers, but in practice it performed
but a few duties in its own name.   The most important assembly was really the *Senate.*   The senators, at first one hundred, later three hundred
in number, were the elders of the patrician order.
Their experience in life fitted them especially for
dealing with public questions, and it was upon
them, therefore, rather than upon the Comitia
Curiata, that the principal legislative duties de-
volved., The patricians who composed the Senate
were picked men of the curies; so that the Senate
may be looked upon as a highly competent executive committee of the former assembly.   The Senate continued to be a leading feature of the Roman
constitution through all its changes, and in its
prime it represented in a high degree the energy
and conservatism of the people, and was probably
the most dignified and able body that the world
has yet known.   From its subordinate position as
a royal council it came to wield a power of its
own, and in the splendid days of the republic the
force and intellect which ruled the city, directed
war, and organized the whole known world into
provinces, was the Roman Senate.*

At the head of the patricians was the king (*rex*).
He was the head of every department of the government.   With the advice, should he require it,
but not necessarily with the consent of the Senate

---

* The official title of the Roman Commonwealth was always SENATUS
POPULUSQUE ROMANUS, "the Senate and the Roman people."   The
abbreviated form of the Latin being S. P. Q. R.

he published his edicts, which were the laws. Representing the citizen body much as the father of a Roman family represented his household, he acted as high-priest and the head of the State religion. Either in his own person or through deputies he presided in the law-courts, and in him rested the supreme command of the army. In all but one important particular point his sway was absolute : his power was derived from, and at his decease returned to, the people—not to his son, nor to any man of his selection. His term of office was for life, and he had no voice in the choice of his successor. When a king died the Senators in turn acted as vice-kings (*inter-reges*) until they could agree upon a new sovereign. The patrician whom the Senate selected had to receive the approval or ordination of the Comitia Curiata, and that body only could confer upon him the *imperium*—the right to rule in the city and the command of the army in the field.

Such seems to have been the primitive government of Rome—two orders dwelling within the same city limits : a ruling order, conducting the business of government through the Comitia, the Senate, and indirectly through one of its own number elevated to almost absolute power as king; the other order composed of freemen, destitute of political rights. Every new advance of Rome swelled the number of the plebeians. Their order gained by every successful war and by every new trader who settled in the city. The patrician order relied only upon natural causes for its growth, and even this increase was retarded by the compulsory military service which subjected the patricians alone to the ravages of frequent campaigns. Excluded by law from camp and court and temple, the ambitious plebeian plunged into trade and agriculture. Roman energy and Roman brains were not the monopoly of the patricians, and there gradually arose among the plebeians a set of men whose achievements in private life encouraged them to ask a share in public affairs. Moreover, it was no easy matter for the small patrician order to bear all the burdens of war. From these two causes came the reform in the government which has been attributed to King Servius Tullius, and which is called the Servian Constitution. In order to divide the patrician military burden with the plebeians, and at the same time to admit the latter in a certain limited sense to an equality with the former, this memorable reform in the composition of the army was introduced. The three historic tribes were abolished and all the land-owning Romans who dwelt within the walls were included in four tribes, according to the region or city ward in which they lived. A census or numbering and valuation of the tribesmen was then taken, and from it a new muster-roll for the army was drawn up. All male property-holders between the ages of seventeen and sixty were divided into five classes. The first class comprised those who owned at least twenty *jugera* of tilled land. These men must present

themselves fully armed, and they were divided
into eighty *centuries* (hundreds or companies) one
half of them liable for field duty, the other half,
composed of older men, being assigned to service
as a reserve. The second class comprised twenty
centuries similarly divided. Only fifteen *jugera*
of land was the standard of admission to this class,
and its members were not compelled to furnish a
full suit of armor. The third, fourth, and fifth
classes were computed on a similar scale. But
the fifth class numbered twenty-eight centuries.
These 168' centuries made up the infantry of the
new army. The cavalry was recruited by levying
twelve new centuries of the wealthiest young
men, both patricians and plebeians, and adding
these to the six patrician centuries of horse which
had served in the old army. These rich *equites*
(knights) cut a considerable figure in the later
history of the city, the knights being always the
representatives of the great capitalists.

In the new army, then, the two orders stood for
the first time side by side. Both were taxed for
its support, both were subjected to its hardships,
both shared its glories. The plebeian, although
still far removed from the right to hold political
office, was at last recognized as of some account
in the State. In the army he might even rise to
the rank of centurion or military tribune, and ex-
ercise authority, petty though it was, over such patricians as chanced to form the rank and file.

This military organization of Servius Tullius

was the source of the first political rights which the plebeians obtained; for to this army, composed of both orders, the king submitted proposals concerning war. There was no debate, probably no formal voting; but in some rude way, by shout or by clash of shield and spear, the people made known their approval or dissent. It was this assembly of the people by centuries which developed into the Comitia Centuriata of republican times, the powerful citizen body which elected most of the magistrates and possessed high legislative authority. Under the kings, however, this assembly was probably devoid of political power beyond the slight degree which has just been referred to, the Senate of elders and the Assembly of the Curies (Comitia Curiata), both thoroughly patrician, being still the recognized legislative bodies.

The first essential change in the form of government sprang not from plebeian oppression, but from the ambition of the kings. The student of the legends has noticed a strain of violence and despotism running through the stories of the later kings. The monarch is no longer the revered judge and priest of the people, but has become a military leader. The throne no longer descends peacefully to the patrician whom the Senate nominates and whom the curies and the gods approve. The monarch contrives that the succession shall remain in his own family or to a man of his own selection. The Tarquins are foreigners, Etruscans, and they

introduce foreign customs, outlandish symbols of
royalty, and seem to have ruled over Etruria as
well as Rome.   From these and other indications
it is concluded that at one time Rome succumbed
to the many attacks of its enemies north of the
Tiber and was forced to accept a foreign ruler.
These Tarquins, the Etruscan kings of Rome, disregarded Senate and patrician assemblies and ruled
as despots.   Their absolute power and their military skill placed Rome at the head of the Latin
towns, but bred dissatisfaction and revolution.
The Tarquins resembled the tyrants who were at
the same time lording it over the cities of Greece,
adorning them with splendors of architecture but
depriving them of their liberties.   This military
despotism ended in revolt.   Lucretia's dishonor and
the patriotism of Brutus may be fictions, but the
fact is indubitable that the citizens rose against
the kings at last, in 509 B. C., the legends say.

The causes of the overthrow of the kings are in
plain sight.   The king had gained his despotic
power at the expense of the patricians.   The plebeians had nothing to lose.   The patricians had been
the State.   King and Senate were of their own
number and governed in their interest.   A usurp-
ing foreign king, who disregarded the advice of
the Senate and treated the curies with contempt,
was intolerable to their order.   The arrogance of
Tarquinius Superbus hastened the crisis.   The
kings were expelled after a long war which weakened the city and degraded it from its leadership

in Latium. But the persistence with which the people maintained the struggle against the Tarquins and their Latin and Etruscan allies is evidence of the sincerity of their hatred. In after times the very name of king was accursed in the city, and there was no surer way of crushing a public man than to spread the report that he aimed to make himself king. The republic which succeeded the monarchy lasted for nearly five hundred years and passed through many changes. Within that time many men strove to seize the chief power in the State, but no man dared to wear the crown. Even Cæsar, who put an end to the republic and was the virtual sovereign of the empire, refused the name of king, in deference, doubtless, to this persistent hatred.

In another chapter we shall see how the patricians endeavored to secure for themselves the sovereignty in the republic.

CHAPTER III.

SECOND PERIOD.

THE ROMAN REPUBLIC. (478 years.)   509–
31 B. C.

THE traditional date of the expulsion of the
Roman kings is 509 B. C., and it is an accepted
fact that the empire was established in the year
31 B. C. Throughout the intervening period of
four hundred and seventy-eight years Rome was a
republic.

The history of these times may be divided for
convenience into three parts ; namely,

I. 509–264 B. C.—The rise of the plebeians in
the city and the rise of Rome in Italy.

II. 264–133 B. C.—The Punic wars and foreign
conquests.

III. 133–31 B. C.—The civil wars. Conquests
abroad. The fall of the republic.

These three divisions will be considered in turn,
and it will be shown how the republican city consolidated its own elements of strength, united Italy
with Roman cement, crushed its civilized rivals—
Carthage, Corinth, Asia—repelled barbarian invasion, conquered the Gauls in their own lands,
and then, in full possession of wealth and power

extraordinary, fell upon times of corruption and civil disorder which ended in the overthrow of the republic by Julius Cæsar, who founded a monarchy to maintain the conquests which the commonwealth had made.

Part I. (509-264 B. C.)

THE RISE OF THE PLEBEIANS IN THE CITY AND THE RISE OF ROME IN ITALY.

The first historian of Rome, Quintus Fabius Pictor, was born after the close of this period, and the modern student is dependent upon histories which were written from three to five centuries after the occurrence of the events which they narrate. Consequently the early chapters of the republic are almost as rich in fanciful legends as were the stories of the kings. The chief sources from which the Roman writers made up their narratives were the annals kept by the priestly colleges, the lists of anniversary holidays, the laws and treaties preserved on metal tablets in the temples, and the private records of the patrician families, who preserved with jealous pride the names of their ancestors who had held high office in the State.

In the histories of Livy and Dionysus this framework of fact is so lavishly upholstered with legendary material that it is often difficult to detect the truth amid its false surroundings. Many of the legends have become familiar in literature, and for that reason some of them will be repeated here, with due warning to the reader.

The period before us has two aspects. At one and the same time two changes were taking place in the Roman State. Within the city her people, patrician and plebeian, were fighting face to face for political equality. Without the walls patricians and plebeians were fighting side by side to extend the authority of the city over the Italian peninsula. In following the two lines of development the scene will change more than once.

The Roman monarchy had been aristocratic. The elective king was a patrician—that is, of "noble" blood ; his council, the Senate, was exclusively patrician ; he was the pope of the patrician priesthood and the leader of the patrician army. The plebeians dwelt in the city, but had no part nor lot in public affairs.

When the Tarquins made themselves absolute rulers the patricians, angry at their loss of influence, headed a revolution and drove out the kings forever. The government which they set up was as thoroughly patrician as its founders dared to make it. The chief magistracy was bestowed upon two patrician consuls of equal authority, who held office for a single year. The chief priesthood was given to a patrician, "king of the sacrifices," and much of the judicial and financial authority fell to two quaestors, also patricians. In case of extreme peril the consul might proclaim a dictator, who was in fact absolute king for the six months, to which his authority was limited. This officer appointed his own lieutenant (*magister equitum*, or "master of the horse"), and was chosen, like the other magistrates, from the patrician order.

The Senate of the earlier period was little changed by the revolution. But its numbers fell off in the wars with the banished kings, and the new consuls filled up the ranks with men from the rich families. It is believed that there were plebeians among the families thus ennobled, but it is uncertain whether the plebeian senators came at once into the full senatorial dignity and privilege.

In the monarchical system there had been but one assembly of the citizens—the Comitia Curiata —based on the triple tribal division into the patrician Ramnes, Tities, and Luceres. In the republic this assembly survived, but its power sank with the rise of the plebeians until it came to deal only with exclusively patrician matters. Besides this ancient Assembly of the Curies two other comitia, or assemblies, grew until they usurped its powers and overshadowed its importance. The elder of these was the Comitia Centuriata, or Assembly of the Centuries. The organization of the land-owning Romans of both orders for military purposes took place under the kings. It was the great feature of the reform of Servius Tullius. In essence it enlarged the body of Roman citizens by admitting to service in the army and to petty military office the land-owning plebeians. The centuries, or hundreds, were at first purely military bands, and had no other voice in affairs of state

than the simplest expression of opinion upon
the question of declaring war. In itself this
was little ; in its possibilities of expansion it was
much ; for it was the first recognition of the political existence of the plebeians. The distribution
of the citizens in the centuries and the methods of
voting gave the rich classes a preponderating influence in this body, so that, although the centuries
included both orders, the ancient aristocracy controlled its action. The military Comitia Centuriata
of Servius became the great popular assembly of
the republic. The right of electing the chief
magistrate was transferred from the curies to the
centuries, and the course of appeal from the consul's death sentence was similarly altered. It was,
perhaps, a little later that the Assembly of the
Centuries actually gained the right of accepting
or rejecting the bills proposed to them by the consul. This right, early secured, made this mixed
assembly a law-making body, or legislature ; but it
differed from most law-making bodies in its composition. It was not a representative body ; its
members were not elected ; every man represented
himself alone, and in theory the Assembly of the
Centuries included every Roman land-owner, the
only distinctions being those of property.

In addition to the old patrician Assembly of the
Curies and the newly enfranchised Assembly of the
Centuries there originated somewhat later a third
and (perhaps) purely plebeian body, the Assembly
of the Tribes, or *Comitia Tributa.* These tribes

were not the three ancient aristocratic divisions, but were rather districts of the city and its suburbs, at first twenty in number, later twenty-one, and finally thirty-five. How this assembly began is extremely doubtful, but it rose with the rise of the plebeians, who constituted its membership, and it ultimately became co-equal in power with the Assembly of the Centuries.

The patricians had been the chief gainers from the expulsion of the kings. They had secured patrician magistrates and generals, a patrician senate and priesthood, and patrician supremacy in the Assembly of the Centuries; even the admission of the plebeians to the army was a gain for the aristocrats. The long struggle with the exiled Tarquins, which the legendary story embellishes with the great deeds of Horatius, Porsena, and Scævola, and which closed with the memorable victory at Lake Regillus, brought great misery to the common soldiers of the lower " classes." They were the owners of small farms, which suffered from the absence of their proprietors in the wars. The soldier served without pay. Debt was inevitable. The Roman law gave the debtor to his creditor as a slave. The booty of successful war went to the State, and, the patricians had the use of its fruits. Public land (*ager publicus*) acquired by conquest was leased to the patrician land-holders, but the rents were carelessly collected, and the patrician to whom the lands were assigned often clung to possession as if they were

5

his by grant or purchase. Great farms grew up, tilled by slave-labor, and the small farmers, between debt and military service, were driven to despair and revolt.

In 494 B. C. the plebeians of the army, returning from a successful campaign, encamped on a height overlooking the junction of the Tiber and Anio rivers, and declared their independence. They determined to rid themselves of patrician oppression by abandoning Rome and founding a plebeian city on the site of their encampment. Their numbers and spirit were a menace to Rome, and the aristocrats were forced to a compromise. The seceders re-entered Rome, but they came as victors. Their debts were forgiven, their revolt went unpunished, and they were given—what they had never had before—magistrates of their own. Plebeians were not admitted to any of the existing offices, but Tribunes of the People (at first, perhaps, only two, like the consuls, afterward five, and still later ten), were given them to preside at plebeian meetings and to champion the rights of the commons at all times and places except in the army. The tribunes were elected by the plebeians themselves, in what assembly at first is doubtful, but after 472 surely in the Comitia Tributa. They had the right of *veto* upon the acts of all magistrates and assemblies. They could not be legally prosecuted during their year of office, and their houses were a legal refuge for plebeians charged with crime. The rights of veto and of protection were enormous concessions on the patrician side, and from this time the contest of the orders was hotly waged. Plebeian ædiles were elected to assist the tribunes and supervise the markets. The hill where the plebeians had encamped was afterward known and honored by that order as the Sacred Mount (*mons sacer*), and the whole episode is called "The First Secession of the Plebs."

In the disorders of the revolution and the secession Rome lost her place at the head of Latium. The legends indicate that the Etruscans were for a time victorious over the Romans, and after their retreat the various tribes of Latium were at war with their former leader. The Latins and the Romans combined against the neighboring Sabines, Æqui, Volsci, and Etruscans, and almost every year had its campaign. Incessant wars again impoverished the plebeians ; and it is said that in a year of famine (491 B. C.) Coriolanus, consul at Rome, sought to induce the plebeians to give up the tribunate in return for free grants of grain from the State. For this and for contempt of court he was banished, and, joining the Volscians, afterward led them against Rome, and would have sacked the town had not his Roman wife and mother saved it by their tearful entreaties. To separate her enemies, the Volsci and Æqui, Rome allied herself to the Hernici (486 B. C.), thus contributing much to the re-establishment of her former strength.

Notwithstanding the concessions of the sacred law the condition of the poorer people of Rome was rendered worse and worse by the incessant wars. Much military duty, with no pay and scanty harvests, drove the farmers into bankruptcy, which meant ruin. The public lands continued in the possession of the patricians or the equally greedy plebeian capitalists. Slaves increased in numbers and the value and dignity of free labor declined. In 486 B. C. Spurius Cassius, consul, proposed a land-law, or " Agrarian law," the first of many by which it was sought to curb the greed of the wealthy Romans. This bill provided that all public lands should be surveyed and a portion of them be leased for the profit of the State. The remainder should be distributed freely among needy citizens of both orders and among the Latin allies. The last clause aroused the jealousy and pride of the Romans. They would admit no Latin to a share in Roman privileges. The cry was raised that the consul was thus purchasing popularity, meaning to make himself king, and the wise man who had generously prescribed the only remedy for the ills of the city was denounced as a traitor, condemned, and executed. So the plebeians gained nothing.

Still there was discord in the city. One patrician family—the Fabii—went into exile to shun the strife, and met death at the brook Cremera at the hands of the Etruscans (477 B. C.). Four years later a tribune was murdered, in spite of his inviolability, because he had used his legal power against two patrician consuls. In 472 B. C. the Publilian

law confirmed the right of the plebeians to elect
their magistrates in the Comitia Tributa, which
was either exclusively plebeian or under plebeian
control. Thus for fifty years the lower order held
what it had gained. But its position was insecure.
The laws were made for and by the patricians,
and in most cases interpreted by patrician magistrates. In 462 B. C. the Tribune Terentilius demanded that the body of unwritten law be revised
by a commission, reduced to its simplest form,
and published so that it might be known and read
of all men. The patricians succeeded in post-
poning this reform for a decade. To pacify the
plebeians they increased the number of tribunes to
ten, and divided the unoccupied grounds on the
Aventine Hill among the poorer families. But the
demand was only deferred, and in 451 B. C. it was
granted. The patricians gave up their consuls
and the plebeians their tribunes, and the consular
power was given for the space of one year to a
committee of ten, the Decemvirs (*Decemviri*),
chosen from the patricians. A second board of
Decemvirs, this time including three plebeians, was
elected for the year 450 B. C. The Decemvirs
formulated a code of twelve laws, which were accepted by the people, and then published on brass
tablets, which were posted in the city square.
These Laws of the Twelve Tables were not new
legislation, but their principles served to fix the
hitherto doubtful or arbitrary decisions of the patrician magistrates, and were thus a great benefit.

The work of the Decemvirs was done, but the enjoyment of power was too sweet to be freely put aside ; accordingly they continued in office in 449 B. C., and with Appius Claudius at their head ruled as tyrants. The legends tell of their murder of Lucius Dentatus, the bravest soldier of Rome, and of the attempted abduction of the fair Virginia by Appius. These outrages led the plebeians to retire to the Sacred Mount, the scene of their former victory. The second secession was equally profitable. The moderate aristocrats effected an arrangement for the re-establishment of consuls and tribunes. The Decemvirs abdicated and died in prison or abroad, and the plebeians returned to Rome (448 B. C.), where the Valerio-Horatian laws still further fortified their position. This legisla- tion (1) endorsed the Laws of the Twelve Tables ; (2) compelled every magistrate to allow a condemned man to appeal to the Assembly of the Centuries ; (3) allowed the tribunes to inflict fines ; (4) established two additional patrician quæstors as treasurers of the military funds ; (5) allowed the tribune to witness the proceedings of the Senate and interpose his veto ; (6) reasserted the inviolability of the tribunes, invoking a curse on their assailants.

Success emboldened the plebeians. They knew their value to the city's prosperity, and their demands grew in number and audacity. In 445 B. C. the law of Canuleius bridged the gulf between the orders by legalizing the marriage of patricians and plebeians.   The same tribune proposed, three quarters of a century in advance of his time, that the consulate be opened to the plebeians.   This was denied; but the patricians devised a make-shift by which the assembly might decide in any year to elect six military tribunes, with consular power, in place of the two patrician consuls. To this new tribunate both orders were eligible. Thus the aristocracy were compelled to grant in reality what they attempted to deny.   They would not admit their rivals to the consulate; but they would not exclude them from the consular tribunate, which had almost equal power.   To save their dignity still farther the patricians established a new office of their own.   Hitherto the consuls had taken the census of the citizens— an enrollment which determined the standing of the individual in the Assembly of the Centuries and in the Senate.   To withhold the control of the Senate from the possibly plebeian influence of the consular tribunes the censorship was created. Two censors, both patricians, were chosen by the centuries, and clothed with power to take the census every five years, and compile the lists of citizens, senators, and knights.   They had the responsible supervision of the State revenues and expenditures, and were charged with the oversight of public morals.

In 421 B. C. the office of quæstor, hitherto pa-trician, was first opened to the plebeians.   This was significant of the end, for it was the first of the

ordinary magistracies for which they were made
eligible. Three of them had been decemvirs and
others had gained consular rank as military tribunes, but they had been debarred the ancient honors which the quæstorship now opened to them.

From 405 to 396 B. C. Rome was engaged in a
duel with Veii, a strong town of southern Etruria.
The war was as fruitful of prodigies as the famous
siege of Troy by the Greeks, and the Romans, who
were eventually successful under the leadership of
Camillus, told wonderful stories of their own heroic deeds. It was in this prolonged campaign
that the citizen soldiery of Rome first received
pay, the army remaining in the field all winter.
The fall of Veii was a heavy blow to Etruscan
prosperity, but her countrymen could neither lend
aid to the city nor avenge its destruction, for
their entire State was threatened by an invasion
from the north. The Gauls, a Germanic tribe,
had long before entered the valley of the Po and
driven the Etruscans into their historic limits.
Hither they followed them, and the aid which
Roman envoys gave to the men of Clusium provoked the barbarians to declare war on Rome itself.
The annals relate that the Gauls routed the Roman
army on the brook Allia, a few miles from Rome,
July 18, 390 B. C. The citizens fled, only a few
remaining to guard the Capitoline temples. The
Gauls burned the city, murdered the steadfast
senators, and, had it not been for the cackling of
Juno's geese, would have surprised and sacked the

citadel. It is believed that Brennus, the Gaulish chief, was bribed to abandon the siege ; but tradition has it that Camillus, "the second founder of Rome," surprised and defeated the besiegers. Then the citizens returned after considering the question of abandoning the ruins and planting a new Rome at Veii. The Gauls proceeded southward, and in the following years often threatened, but never took, the city. At last they settled in the Po valley and adopted the Roman civilization.

The long war with the people of Veii and the disastrous inroads of the plundering Gauls increased the miseries of the poorer citizens and hastened the means of relief. The debt and destitution of the plebeian poor touched the hearts of individuals in both orders. In 439 B. C. Spurius Mælius, a plebeian, was killed by Ahala, a high officer, for distributing grain to the needy. The patricians slew him for his ambition. In 384 B. C., Manlius, who had kept the Capitoline against the Gauls, was thrown from its cliffs as a punishment for paying the debts of bankrupt plebeians. The patricians said he wanted to be king. But isolated executions could not suppress the popular cry for equal political rights and equal justice in regard to the public lands. In 376 B. C. the popular demand took form in the propositions of the tribunes, Licinius and Sextius, which in 367 B. C. were accepted by the assembly and became the famous Licinian laws.

It was enacted : (1) That the office of consular-

military tribune should be abolished, and that at
least one of the two annually elected consuls must
be a plebeian ; (2) that plebeians should be admitted to priesthoods of a certain class.   These two
laws equalized the political status of the two orders and realized one of the objects for which the
plebeians had battled since 510 B. C.   Furthermore (3) it was enacted that no one should occupy
more than a certain share of the common pasture-
lands or till more than three hundred acres of the
State domain ; (4) that freemen, as well as slaves,
must be employed on every estate ; and (5) that
interest already paid on debts should be deducted
from the principal.

The patricians made futile attempts to nullify
this legislation.   As they had established the
censorship to keep certain privileges away from
the plebeian military tribunes, they now created a
new office, the prætorship.   The prætor, who must
be a patrician, was to act as consul in the absence
of those magistrates, and was at all times to act
as a judge in the highest court of the city.   Two
curule ædiles, also patricians, were likewise appointed to manage the Roman games and public
markets.   But these offices did not long remain
the exclusive property of the old aristocracy.   One
after another they were yielded to the commons.
The Licinian law legalized plebeian consuls; in 356
B. C. the dictatorship was opened to plebeians; in
351 B. C. the restrictions were removed from the
censorship; in 339 B. C. the Publilian law ordered

that one of the censors must be a plebeian ; in
337 B. C. the commons were made eligible to the
prætorship ; in 300 B. C. the Ogulnian law admitted plebeians to office in the priestly colleges of
the augurs and pontifices ; and in 287 B. C. the
Hortensian law, brought about by the third secession of the plebs, established the decrees of the
plebeian Assembly of Tribes (*Comitia Tributa*), as
of equal authority with the laws passed by the
whole body of citizens in the Assembly of the
Centuries (*Comitia Centuriata*).

The Licinian law, with its sequels, the Publilian,
Ogulnian and Hortensian laws, broke down the bar
which had divided the Roman orders. The distinction still survived in the pride of the patrician
families, but in politics the orders were equal. All
the honors of State and Church were open to the
plebeians ; the resolutions of their assembly were
the laws of the State; their consuls led the armies;
their senators sat and voted with the representatives of the ancient houses. The enormous changes
which this chapter summarizes came to pass through
a period of two hundred years. Considered in the
aggregate they represent a complete revolution in
the Roman constitution. It is the spectacle of a
subject class extorting not only liberty but privilege and power from its superiors, and gaining an
equal share in the government. Similar results
have been achieved in other countries, notably in
France, but the Romans alone possessed that political faculty which secured this revolution without

anarchy. The struggle for the equalization of the
orders was fiercely contested, but it was fought in
legal forms, not with fire and sword, and the many
years that preceded its consummation were so many
years of education in those qualities of self-control
which enabled the new Rome to master the world.

While the constitution of the city was in this
stage of its development (367–287 B. C.) Rome
was engaged in a series of wars. She had no
longer to fight for her existence. Her supremacy
in Latium was again recognized as it had been in
the times of the kings, and she made leagues of
equality with the Latins and Hernicans. Until
the wandering Gauls settled themselves upon the
plains of Lombardy their forays brought them into
frequent contact with the Romans, but they never
again approached the walls of the city. With the
repulse of the Gauls, and the submission of the
Latin and Hernican towns, three rival national-
ities under Rome remained in the peninsula. In
closest contact were the Etruscans, weakened by
the loss of Veii and suffering from Gaulish raids.
West and south of Rome were the Italians (see p.
22), of whom the Samnites, rude farmers though
they were, were the leading division. Related to
the Samnites were the Volsci and Æqui, whose
lands adjoined the Latins. The third people were
the Hellenes of Magna Grecia ; luxurious, cultured, and indolent, abounding in resources but
deficient in patriotism, and cursed by the political
incapacity of their race. In one hundred years

(375-275 B. C.) Rome mastered all three races— Etruscan, Samnite, and Greek.

Etruria was in disorder, and its cities fell one by one until the entire southern section of the country, with the cities of Tarquinii, Cære, and Falerii, was subject to Rome (351 B. C.). It was, perhaps, this success which led Carthage, the African city which was then one of the great powers of the world, to form a treaty with the victor (348 B. C.). Rome's next campaigns (350–345 B. C.) were against the Volscians and their kindred Italians on the south, and resulted in a further extension of Roman power. In these campaigns the Roman military formation was re-organized. The infantry of the legion was divided into thirty maniples of three centuries each. These fought in triple line of battle, the first two rows being armed with sword and spear, the third with long lances.

The Roman power, which had suffered much from Gaul and Tuscan, was now in the ascendant. The support of her alliance was now sought by distant tribes. A treaty of this sort precipitated the inevitable struggle with the Samnites. Two truces divide the conflict into the three Samnite wars. The first was of little importance. Beginning in 343 B. C. with an alliance between Rome and Capua, it lasted till 341 B. C., when the Samnites were distracted by a Greek attack in their rear and the Romans by a revolt of the Latins. Rome gained the pleasant city of Capua in the settlement.

The Latin war (340–338 B. C.) was the protest
of the Latin towns against Roman exclusiveness.
Romans and Latins had fought side by side as
allies, but Rome had claimed the spoils of the victory. The city was prospering and growing in
power and wealth, and the Latins demanded a
share in its government. They saw the first triumphs of the plebeians, and they raised a cry for
equal recognition in the affairs of the city. But
it was a fundamental doctrine of the Roman republic to restrict as far as possible the rights of
citizenship to actual inhabitants of the city. The
war resulted in the complete victory of the Romans;
the Latin league was dissolved. Its cities made
separate treaties with Rome and were cut off from
direct intercourse with each other. Roman garrison towns (colonies) were planted among them
and the Latin State was at an end.

In 326 B. C. the second Samnite war began.
It lasted, with varying fortunes, until 305 B. C.,
and involved nearly all the nations of the peninsula. The mountaineers were led by the Samnite,
Gavius Pontius, who (321 B. C.) entrapped both
the consular armies in the pass near Caudium,
known as the "Caudine Forks," and compelled the
consuls to accept a treaty, which, however, the
Senate rejected. The Etruscans took sides with
the Samnites (in 312 B. C.), but were beaten at
the Vadimonian Lake (310 B. C.). Gradually
the Samnites were deprived of their allies, and in
305 B. C. their capital, Bovianum, surrendered

to the Romans. Peace was made on equal
terms.

Although the Romans had gained in these wars
their stubborn foe was by no means subjugated.
Rome occupied the seven years which elapsed before the third outbreak by strengthening her own
position. In Latium she forced the subject tribes
to accept a form of citizenship which was like that
of the plebeians two centuries earlier. They were
citizens *without suffrage*—that is, they served in
Roman armies and paid taxes to Rome, but could
not vote in the city assemblies nor hold Roman
office. Throughout the conquered territory that
peculiar institution, the Roman colony, was
planted. Roman citizens, soldiers with their
wives and children, were assigned lands near the
conquered towns, and removed thither. These
colonists retained their full rights as citizens of
Rome, and when in the mother city might vote
in the assemblies. In their new homes they were
not only garrisons, but centers of Roman influence in every way, contributing to the extension
of Latin language and Roman law, by which the
races of the peninsula were brought into union.
To facilitate communication between the scattered
colonies, and to furnish means for the rapid transportation of troops, the Senate authorized the con-
struction of a grand system of military roads.
These perfect highways, some of which may yet
be traced, were extended as fast as the conquests
permitted. Before the third Samnite war a large

part of the Appian Way (*via Appia*), which was
to connect Rome and Brundisium, was built, and
two northern roads, the Flaminian and Valerian,
were constructed into the heart of the Samnite
mountains.

The mountaineers perceived the significance of
these operations, and formed alliances with the
Etruscans and Gauls of the north and the southern
Italians, preparatory to a decisive struggle against
Rome. The third Samnite war lasted from 298
B. C. to 290 B. C., and the Romans won by strik-
ing the members of the league in turn before they
could unite. In the great battle of Sentinum the
Gauls and Samnites were defeated by the Roman
consuls. The allies fell away, but the Samnites
held out five years longer, until 290 B. C. They
gained honorable terms of peace, but were so
weakened that they no longer stood between Rome
and the supremacy of Italy.

The Roman conquests were rapidly secured by
strong colonies and fine roads. Roman influences
had now reached southern Italy, and a three-years'
war, with an alliance of Italian tribes (285–282
B. C.), ended in the partial destruction of the
Gaulish Senones and the establishment of Roman
garrisons in several cities of Great Greece. Tarentum, a proud and wealthy city of this neighborhood, jealous of the Roman advance, attacked
a Roman fleet and led to war (282 B. C.). Pyrrhus, the King of Epirus, came with elephants and
a great army to aid the Tarentine Greeks. The

Romans refused to yield, though dismayed by the force which confronted them. Their army was beaten at Heraclea (280 B. C.), and again at Asculum (279 B. C.). But the result was indecisive. The Roman allies joined Pyrrhus, but the Romans resisted heroically. "Another such victory," said Pyrrhus, "and I am undone." Affairs in Sicily demanded the presence of the king, and on his return he found the Roman position greatly strengthened. In the battle of Beneventum (275 B. C.) he was utterly defeated. Pyrrhus then left Magna Grecia at the mercy of Rome. Tarentum surrendered (272 B. C.), and the Samnites and other tribes who had broken their treaties were severely punished. By the year 264 B. C. all Italy, from the Rubicon to the Straits of Messina and the Ionian Sea, was subject to Rome.

In this united Italy the citizens of Rome were the governing body. Outside of Rome there were three general classes of communities—the colonies, whose citizens were still full citizens of Rome; the municipalities (*municipia*), whose citizens, like the early plebeians, bore the burdens of Roman citizenship, the taxes and liability to military service, but could neither vote at Rome nor hold a Roman office ; and the allies, or *socii*, who were bound to Rome by treaties upon various terms of dependence.

The first period of the Roman Republic began with the expulsion of the kings, 509 B. C., and ended with the unification of Italy, 264 B. C. The

6

political character of the people was now formed,
their military organization improved, and their
triumph over Pyrrhus and the Greeks encouraged
them in the contest about to open with Carthage
for the supremacy of the Mediterranean Sea.

CHAPTER IV.

SECOND PERIOD (Continued).

THE ROMAN REPUBLIC.

Part II. (264–133 B. C.)

THE PUNIC WARS AND FOREIGN CONQUESTS.

AT the beginning of the second period of the republic Rome was confronted by her first foreign rival, Carthage. Tyre and Sidon, the famous coast cities of Canaan or Phenicia, planted their trading colonies at many points on the Mediterranean before 1000 B. C. There are distinct traces of Phenician influence in Greece, and the Bible testifies to the boldness of their commercial enterprises. Among the Phenician—in Roman language "Punic"—settlements in the western seas Carthage easily gained and held the first rank. The situation, near that of the modern city of Tunis, was most advantageous for a center of trade, and the Tyrians who settled there made the most of their opportunity. Carthage became the head of a North African empire ; her fleets ruled the Western Mediterranean and visited Britain, and her own trading colonies abounded in Sicily, Sardinia, and Spain, as well as along the African

coast. The city demanded tribute from every de-
pendency and filled the ranks of her armies with
mercenary troops. Only the generals were
Carthaginians, and the patriotism which animated
the Roman common soldier was unknown among
the Libyans and Numidians who fought in the pay
of the African city. Carthage was governed by
an oligarchy of wealthy merchants. There was no
prosperous middle class of citizens, the whole State
being made up of capitalists, of landless freemen,
and of slaves, myriads of whom cultivated the
plantations and handled the goods of the merchant
princes.

A comparison between Rome and Carthage at
the outbreak of the war is favorable to the former.
Rome was far poorer in money and material resources, and far less civilized, but she had the support of united Italy, whose people were related to
each other and bound to herself by the expectation
of some share in the glory and profits of her greatness. Carthage had enormous wealth and was invincible on the sea ; but her land army was composed of hired or impressed subjects, not of freemen, and her dependencies hated her as a monop-
olist of trade and a greedy collector of tribute.

The duel between Rome and Carthage began in
Sicily, and in this wise : A band of ruffians from
Magna Grecia, calling themselves " Sons of Mars "
seized the citadel of Messana, in Sicily, and held it
against the assaults of Hiero II., king of the Greek
city Syracuse, who sought to dislodge them. In

their extremity they asked aid of the Romans, who
had as yet no foothold in the islands, and of the
Carthaginians, who had more than a score of
colonies there. The Roman Senate hesitated to
send an army out of Italy, and Carthage, by
prompt action, got possession of the town before
the consul's army crossed the straits. But the

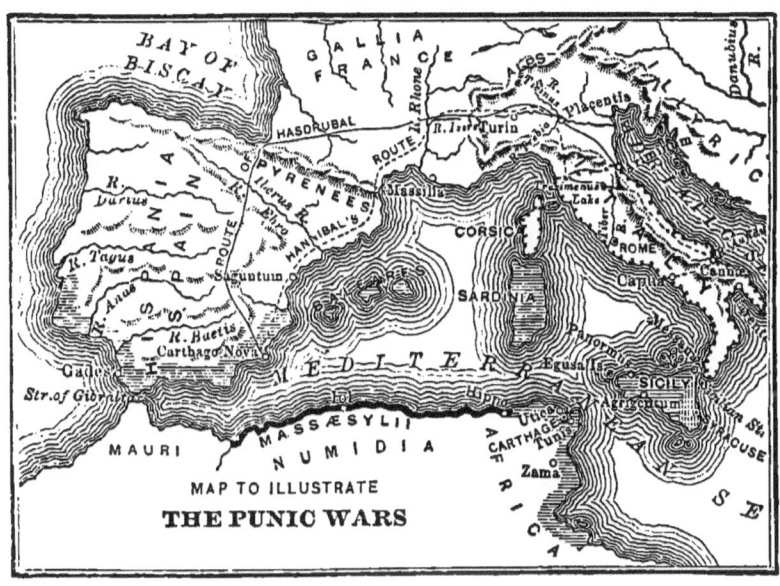

MAP TO ILLUSTRATE

THE PUNIC WARS

Romans drove out the Carthaginian garrison and
occupied Messana for themselves. Carthage thereupon declared war (264 B. C.). Rome had the
advantage during the first eight years of the contest. Hiero attached himself to her, and their
united forces made short work of the interior
towns. Agrigentum, also, was taken after a long
siege; but there the Roman conquests were stayed.

The strong coast fortresses were safe from her land attacks, and Rome had no navy worthy of the name. The Senate resolved to supply the deficiency; indeed, a fleet was necessary not only for offensive purposes, but to protect the defenseless Italian harbors. A Carthaginian five-decker (*quinquereme*), beached on the Latin coast, furnished a model, and in 260 B. C. the energy of the Romans equipped a fleet of one hundred and twenty large vessels of war. To offset their rude seamanship they crowded their galleys with fighting men and provided grappling-irons and boarding bridges by which their soldiers might come to close combat with the Carthaginian marines. The

Caius Duilius.

device worked admirably, and Caius Duilius won Rome's first naval battle with their aid, in this same year, 260 B. C., at Mylæ, near Messana. The fleet seized several towns on the shores of Sicily and Corsica ; but Panormus, Drepanum, and Lilybæum resisted stoutly, and Hamilcar, the Carthaginian general in Sicily, even won back some of the inland cities. In order to stop this desultory warfare the Roman Senate fitted out a fleet of three hundred and thirty ships for an attack upon Carthage itself. A Punic fleet of equal numbers was beaten at Ecnomus, and

(256 B. C.) the Romans landed a few miles from
the great city.   Overconfidence induced them to
send back a portion of the ships and soldiers, leaving the Consul Marcus Atillius Regulus in command.   The city would have fallen had the consul
been energetic ; but his terms of surrender were
too exacting, and before he was ready to strike
defenders were summoned.   Hamilcar hastened
from Sicily with his veterans, and Greek infantry
and Numidian horsemen were hired in multitudes.
Xanthippus came from Sparta to superintend the
military operations.   The Spartan cut the Roman
legions to pieces with his cavalry and elephants,
and took the consul captive (255 B. C.).   The fleet
which the Romans sent to bring off the remnant of
the army was shattered in a storm.

There is an interesting Roman
story, of doubtful veracity, that
Regulus was sent to Rome with
a Carthaginian embassy to treat
for peace.   It was supposed that
the captive would use his influence for a cessation of hostilities
and his own release.   But the
proud   and   patriotic   Roman
begged his fellow senators to

Marcus Atillius Reg-
ulus.

prosecute the war with all their might and so
avenge the disgrace of his defeat.   Then he went
back to his prison in Carthage, and his captors
avenged their disappointment by inflicting upon
him a cruel death (250 B. C.).

The African campaign was a failure, and Sicily again became the scene of war. Panormus capitulated to Rome (254 B. C.). Storms had again wrecked a Roman fleet (255 B. C.) and disgusted the Senate with naval warfare. On the land success was rare. In 251 B. C. the Consul Metellus defeated Hasdrubal near Panormus, but two years later the Carthaginians destroyed the remnant of the Roman sea force. Active operations now languished ; but Hamilcar, surnamed Barca, " The Lightning," from his fierce and unexpected attacks, maintained himself in Sicily, harassing the consuls and playing havoc with the allies of Rome and Syracuse. The Roman merchants, whose trade had declined in consequence of the exhausting war, raised a naval fund and presented it to the State. The Consul Lutatius Catulus was assigned to the command of the new fleet, which won the decisive battle of the Ægusan Islands (241 B. C.). This closed the first Punic war. The treaty of peace awarded to Rome all the Carthaginian possessions in Sicily and a war indemnity of $4,000,000 to be paid within ten years.

Neither Rome nor Carthage was idle in the twenty-three years which elapsed between the first and second Punic wars. Rome's first care was to strengthen her defenses. Italy proper was already bound to her. She now organized her Sicilian conquest into a province—the first of many foreign possessions. Sardinia, also, was won over from Carthage, and combined with

Corsica to form a second province. Affairs in the west being satisfactorily composed, the Senate—now a body of great wisdom and executive force—turned its attention to the east and north. The Illyrian pirates, whose haunts were among the inlets and islets of the eastern border of the Adriatic, and who had troubled the commerce of Italy and preyed upon the coast cities of Greece, were thoroughly chastised between the years 229 B. C. and 219 B. C. The Greek towns, relieved from their fears, admitted their Roman liberators to share their national games and religious rites. It was a dangerous guest that they summoned to their feast.

Another invasion by the restless Gauls from the Po valley aroused the Romans to the necessity of subjugating these turbulent northern neighbors. They were beaten 225 B. C. in the battle of Telamon, and driven back from Etruria into Cisalpine Gaul. Here the Romans planted important colonies—Placentia, Cremona, Mutina—and extended the Flaminian military road to this region. These measures were scarcely completed when the Carthaginians precipitated the second Punic war.

After her first encounter with Rome Carthage had come under the influence of a great man. Hamilcar Barca, the dashing leader who had delayed the Roman conquest of Sicily, was keen enough to see that there was an irrepressible conflict of interest between the two great cities. Carthage had lost Sicily, and he endeavored to

build up in Spain another and richer province, to
offset the loss, and to supply resources upon which
to draw in time of necessity. The Carthaginians
granted him an army and dictatorial power, and
with these he crossed over to Spain (238 B. C.).
By his skill as a general and his ability as a
statesman he established a rich and powerful
Spanish State, dependent upon Carthage. When
he fell in battle (228
B. C.) his son-in-law,
Hasdrubal,   contin-
ued the work. Rome
took alarm and fixed
the river Iberus
(Ebro) as the east-
ward limit of Carth-
aginian conquest;
but no aggressive
action was taken un-
til Hasdrubal was
too strong to be put
down. When an as-

Hannibal.

sassin's dagger ended his life (220 B. C.), the command of the Carthaginians in Spain fell into yet
more efficient hands. When Hamilcar Barca left
Carthage on his Spanish errand he called to the
altar his eldest son, Hannibal, a boy of nine years,
and made him swear a solemn oath to cherish undying hatred toward Rome. This boy served with
his father and brother-in-law in the western campaigns, and won favor with the soldiers. He was

twenty-eight years old when Hasdrubal died, and the army hailed him as its leader. He perceived that the time for which his father had prepared was now at hand. The Spanish kingdom was firmly established, and its revenues not only paid the expense of government and conquest, but yielded a surplus to the treasury of the mother-city. The army which had accomplished this work was not the usual mercenary medley which fought for Carthage. Its men had been hardened by long campaigns, inspirited by repeated successes under Hamilcar and Hasdrubal ; they were well-paid and well-fed veterans, devoted to their leader and fired with his own enthusiasm. Hannibal himself was the central figure of the war. He was one of the greatest commanders of history, and his talent far transcended that of a mere leader of troops. He was a statesman of foresight and energy, and until he died Rome trembled at his name.

To break the peace Hannibal sacked Saguntum, a town under Roman protection, and disregarded the limits which Rome had fixed. The envoys of the Senate demanded the surrender of Hannibal ; Carthage refused, and war was declared 218 B. C.

The second Punic war was not a succession of futile and desultory campaigns like the first, but was conducted by Hannibal upon a carefully elaborated plan. He saw that the strength of Rome rested in her allies—that united Italy was his real foe. To deprive the city of its allies would be its

ruin. The Cisalpine Gauls were still in angry
mood from their chastisement and from the erection of the military colonies on their lands in the
Po valley. There were men still living in Samnium and Etruria who could remember when their
countries were free from the Roman yoke, and
who still regretted their lost liberty. The Greek
towns of southern Italy were but slightly bound
to the city which had conquered them only fifty
years before. These considerations determined
Hannibal's plan of attack. He would enter northern Italy with all speed, call the disaffected Gauls
to his standard, and then march southward in the
guise of a liberator, seducing Etruscans, Samnites
and Greeks from their Roman allegiance. Having
shorn Rome of her allies he would crush her
legions with his veteran troops. We shall see how
closely this design was followed and with what
success.

Having made provision for the defense of Spain
and Africa, Hannibal set out in the spring of 218
B. C. on his famous march. He chose the land
route to Italy, his road crossing south-eastern
Spain, the Pyrenees Mountains, and southern
France. He had 90,000 infantry, 12,000 cavalry,
and 37 elephants; but when he reached the river
Rhone the force had been reduced by hardships
and garrison detachments to 50,000 infantry and
9,000 cavalry, the flower of an army which had
been trained by twenty years of fighting. The
sluggish Roman general, Publius Cornelius Scipio,

was out-maneuvered, and the Carthaginian army crossed the Rhone in safety and made its way to the Alps unmolested. It was September. The mountaineers were hostile and the autumn snows had begun; but Hannibal pressed on over the Little St. Bernard pass, and with the loss of half his foot-soldiers and one third of his mounted men descended to the plains of the Po in Cisalpine Gaul.

The Romans were taken by surprise. The two consular armies which had been sent, the one to Spain, the other to Africa, were recalled in all haste. The Gauls fulfilled Hannibal's expectations by crowding to his head-quarters and enlisting for the war. By the time the northern army under Publius Scipio was ready to face him his troops were rested and half Cisalpine Gaul was at his back. The two armies met (218 B. C.) in the battle of Ticinus, to the discomfiture of the Romans; although the masterly retreat of the wounded Scipio across the Po checked Hannibal's progress. But the advantage was lost by the other consul, Sempronius, who was enticed into the battle of Trebia (218 B. C.), which resulted in the defeat of the Romans and the complete submission of the Cisalpine Gauls. The fortified Roman colonies, however, did not yield, and Hannibal could not stop for sieges. Adhering to his plans he lingered in the north only to the end of winter, and then hastened over the Apennines to Etruria and Italy proper. His coming was heralded by the Italian captives whom he had taken at Trebia and Ticinus and released with honors to scatter the news of his approach. He proclaimed himself the liberator of the Italian towns, and showed them great consideration. But his Roman captives were punished with cruel severity. Thus he sought to impress upon the people that his war was against Rome alone, and that the Italians would find security in alliance with him.

The Carthaginians sickened in great numbers from the malaria of the Etruscan swamps, and Hannibal lost an eye from a disease contracted there. But the Romans, cursed with incompetent leaders, offered no opposition until these ills were over and the enemy reached firm ground again. Then the new consul, who had stayed in camp at Arretium while the enemy were laboring down the other border of the peninsula, gave chase. The Romans came up with the Carthaginians in a defile near Lake Trasimenus and marched into a trap which Hannibal had laid. Fifteen thousand Romans fell and half as many were taken prisoners in this disaster, which can hardly be called a battle. (217 B. C.) Rome stood aghast. All Etruria was lost; Hannibal might march to the Tiber unopposed; but there was no demand for peace. Quintus Fabius Maximus was appointed dictator and a new army of defense was levied.

Some have wondered that Hannibal did not follow up his success at Lake Trasimenus with an attack on Rome. But his plan was wiser. The cavalry which won his battles could not take a walled city, and his army was not prepared for a long siege in the heart of a hostile country.   So he turned eastward to gather forage and plunder in Umbria and Picenum, and to drill and discipline the masses of raw Gallic volunteers who flocked to him.

The dictator Fabius had learned a lesson from the three defeats of his predecessors.   He had not the cavalry nor the skill to defeat the invader in battle; but he hoped to defeat his plans without fighting.   Hannibal had been in Italy two years, but, excepting the Gauls, hardly a single ally of Rome had deserted what surely resembled a losing cause.   The Roman political system and the colonial "patches of Rome" held the subject countries to their fealty.   Hannibal's schemes depended upon breaking this allegiance, and the longer he stayed in Italy without doing so the weaker his position became.   So Fabius followed the invader instead of confronting him.   The eager Roman mob denounced him as *cunctator* ("delayer"), and clamored against him at the news of Hannibal's raids in the rich Campanian farm lands.   His dictatorship expired without a decisive engagement, and two consuls, the hare-brained Varro and the cautious Paulus, were elected for the year 216 B. C.   The defect of the Roman consular system hastened the catastrophe.   The two generals had equal authority, and it was accordingly agreed that each should be supreme on alternate days.

The army, with its alternating commanders, was posted in Apulia watching Hannibal. The impetuous Varro, tired of "Fabian" tactics, gave battle in the open plain of Cannæ, on the little river Aufidus. The level ground was perfectly adapted for the evolutions of the African horse. The legions fought with their usual stubborn energy, but they were out-generaled, surrounded, and their lines broken. Seventy thousand Romans fell victims to Varro's headstrong folly.

That the government of Rome withstood the shock of this disaster was prophetic of the outcome of the war. Capua now joined Hannibal. The Samnites and Lucanians broke their treaty pledges, and sent re-enforcements to the invader. But the great body of the Italians clung to Rome. Scarcely a colony wavered. Hannibal had struck his heaviest blow; he could not surpass the successes at Trebia, Trasimenus, and Cannæ; yet the political unity of Italy was unbroken. At this period Rome deserved the confidence of her allies. There was no suggestion of defeat in the proud spirit of the Senate. Little time was wasted in lamentation for the dead, but every freeman of military age was impressed for the war, and even slaves were armed. Fabius, Gracchus, and Marcellus led the new levies and continued the war in Italy. In Spain the brothers Publius and Cneius Scipio engaged young Hasdrubal, and prevented him from aiding his brother, Hannibal. Carthage sent scanty re-enforcements. Philip, King of

Macedonia, promised much; Rome took care that he should perform little. Hieronymus of Syracuse lent but feeble co-operation. Hannibal's cause declined steadily after Cannæ. The cohesion of the Roman State, the revived energy of Senate and citizens, delayed the consummation of his plans; and delay meant decay. In 215 B. C. he lost his first battle at Nola. The Romans kept Philip occupied by the indecisive first Macedonian war (215–206 B. C.), and Marcellus punished Hieronymus of Sicily by the war which ended in the siege and capture of Syracuse (212 B. C.).

From 212 B. C. to 207 B. C. Hannibal remained comparatively inactive. He captured and lost individual cities, but made no real progress toward the realization of his project. In the year 210 B. C., Publius Cornelius Scipio, a son of the old consul, went to Spain to crush the Carthaginians there. He was fortunate, but Hasdrubal eluded him, 208 B. C., and hastened across the Alps with re-enforcements. The consuls of 207 B. C. were Livius and Nero. The former was in the north of Italy with an army; the latter, in the south, was dogging Hannibal's track, and endeavoring to prevent a junction of the two sons of Hamilcar Barca. By a forced march Nero joined Livius on the Metaurus, defeated and destroyed the auxiliaries under Hasdrubal, and returned to his position in front of Hannibal before that general was aware of his brother's presence in Italy. The loss of the Spanish re-enforcements was disheart-

7

ening; Hannibal retired to Bruttium and abandoned aggressive operations.

Rome now became the attacking party. The
young Scipio returned from Spain in 206 B. C. He
had utterly subdued the kingdom which Hannibal's
father had established there. In 205 B. C. he was
made consul, and prepared "to carry the war into
Africa," as the best means of dislodging the enemy from Italy. With the enthusiastic support
of the Senate he assumed control of the military
operations. One army covered the movements of
Mago, Hamilcar's youngest son, who had landed
in northern Italy; but the greater armament sailed
for Carthage (204 B. C.). The next year Hannibal was recalled to Africa, but the resources of
his city were already exhausted. Scipio defeated
him at Zama (202 B. C.) and closed the war.

Carthage bought peace dearly. She gave up all
claim to her former dominions outside of Africa,
transferred the tributary kingdom of Numidia to
Massinissa, an ally of Rome, destroyed her war
fleet, and bound herself to pay an annual tribute.
The Romans greeted Scipio with extraordinary
honors, and gave him the name "Africanus," in
memory of his triumph.

The close of the war left Rome with many
things to do. Those Greek and Italian cities that
had sided with Hannibal she disgraced and humil-
iated by deprivation of lands and political rights.
Pleasant Capua, the second city of Italy, was
made desolate. The Cisalpine Gauls were re-sub-

jugated and fettered by means of roads and colonies (200–191 B. C.). In Spain there were constant wars, but the country was parceled into two Roman provinces under the government of prætors.

The dethronement of Carthage made Rome the leading power in the Mediterranean, and her relations with eastern nations soon involved her in wars which widely extended her conquests beyond the Adriatic.

Many circumstances prepared the way for an easy conquest of the East. Civilization was at the flood in the countries at the eastern end of the Mediterranean, but power was at a low ebb. Macedonia, Greece, and Syria were the three most important divisions. Their condition at the close of the war with Hannibal will explain their subsequent history. Macedonia was a country of Europe skirting the northern shore of the Ægean Sea. Under two kings, Philip (339–336 B. C.) and Alexander the Great (336–323 B. C.), it had risen from obscurity to the mastery of three quarters of the world. At Alexander's death the empire was divided among a number of his generals, some of whom were capable rulers, who built up the prosperous kingdoms of the Ptolemies in Egypt, of the Seleucidæ in Syria, of Pergamon and Bithynia in Asia Minor, and Macedonia, the old home territory. The three last-named were among the weaker nations, and Macedonia, especially, soon lost its leading place. Greece had been the first conquest

of Alexander's father, Philip, and had exhausted
itself in efforts to regain its freedom. The cities
of Greece bound themselves loosely together in
two leagues, the Ætolian and the Achæan, with
the object of expelling Macedonian garrisons from
their citadels. But these leagues were engaged
in almost continual disputes with each other, and,
despite their patriotic aims, really contributed to
the downfall of the nation by dividing and con-
suming its strength.

The kingdom of Syria was for a time the most
powerful segment of Alexander's empire. It comprised the eastern half of Asia Minor and the
whole of Persia. At the close of the second
Punic war its ruler, Antiochus the Great (224–187
B. C.), was in his prime. He had added many
provinces to his dominions, had adorned his capital, Antioch, with every magnificence, and had
decked his court with all the lavish splendor which
had formerly distinguished the royal households of
Darius and Xerxes, the famous Persians. Like
those conquerors, Antiochus assumed the title of
" King of Kings," or " The Great King," and ex-
acted slavish submission from his people. It was
with declining Macedonia, distressed Greece, and
luxurious Syria that Rome came in contact about
the beginning of the second century before Christ.

The statesmanship of Hannibal had prompted
him to form a league of all the Mediterranean nations in opposition to Rome, and one of his most
promising alliances had been with Philip V., King

of Macedon, whom the success at Cannæ (216 B. C.) won to the Carthaginian side. But the exertions of Rome nullified his good intentions. The Senate sent a small force into Greece and involved the Ætolian league in war against Philip. This first Macedonian war (215–206 B. C.), while not in itself decisive, served Rome's purpose, for it held one enemy in play and enabled the hard-pressed Senate to concentrate all its forces against Hannibal, its mortal foe. The close of this war did not affect the independent relations of the two nations. Philip was left free, but his use of his liberty soon involved him in a second war. He was a bold, restless spirit, endowed with much genius, but cursed with periods of weakness and inaction. Before the battle of Zama he re-opened his alliance with Carthage, and after the peace he attacked Greek cities which the Illyrian pirate-hunting expeditions had made friendly to Rome. On these grounds the Senate decided upon war (200 B. C.). The two Grecian leagues joined the Romans and drove the Macedonians out of Central Greece. Philip made a stand in Thessaly, but was routed at Cynoscephalæ (197 B. C.) by the Consul Titus Quintius Flamininus. The terms of peace included the practical disarmament of the Macedonians. Their treasury was emptied by a heavy war tribute, their land and naval forces were cut down to insignificance, and their foreign policy was placed under Roman direction.

The part which the Greeks had taken in these

campaigns won the friendship of the Romans, and
one of the first acts of the victorious Flamininus
was to declare the independence of the Greek
cities. This was done at the national festival of
the Isthmian games (197 B. C.) amid great rejoic-
ings, which were, perhaps, uncalled for ; for this
" independence " really meant nothing more than
relief from Macedonian supremacy and real dependence upon Rome. The cities were left to
themselves ; the Achæan league was, perhaps,
encouraged ; but the Romans took care that no
foreign influence except their own should dom-
inate the Greek cantons and that no united Greek
nation should acquire a dangerous degree of
power.

After the disaster at Zama, Hannibal, whom the
magnanimity of Scipio had spared, devoted himself
to the rehabilitation of his country. He penetrated
to the defects of its political system with the same
incisive vision which had directed his campaigns
and had struck at the weaknesses of his enemies.
Although defeated he was a popular hero, and
wielded a power in Carthage which Rome wisely
feared. His opponents in the former city accused
him before the Roman Senate, and that body was
willing enough to stay his reforms and banish their
author. Hannibal escaped with his life. The oath
which his boyish lips had sworn in the presence of
his glorious father and the solemn Phenician altars
he had cherished religiously. His hatred of Rome
was undying, and when his own city closed its

gates against him and his efforts to re-organize her resources were thwarted, he clung to his single purpose, the destruction of Rome.   The court of Antiochus the Great was his natural refuge (194 B. C.) He won the favor of the great king, who had not yet come in conflict with the conquering city of the West.   Hannibal engaged the king in his projects of revenge.   Together they planned an anti-Roman coalition of Greeks and Asiatics.   Rome deemed the monarch's reception of Hannibal and his negotiations with the "independent" Greeks a sufficient ground for hostilities, and the so-called " War with Antiochus " began in 192 B. C.

The war opened with a Syrian invasion of Greece (192 B. C.); but the Greek cities, with Macedon and Pergamon, helped the Romans to scatter the king's army.   In 190 B. C. Roman and Rhodian fleets defeated Hannibal's armada at the Eurymedon.   The Roman forces in Asia Minor were commanded by the Consul Lucius Scipio, assisted by his brother, the victor of Zama; they ended the war by the battle of Magnesia (190 B. C.).   Antiochus gave up his possessions in Europe and the western part of his Asiatic provinces, and paid a war indemnity.   Hannibal escaped, but the hatred of Rome followed him to the Bithynian court, and in 183 B. C. he took his own great life by a draught of poison.   Scipio, his conqueror, died at about the same time, an exile by choice from his native city, where his later years had been clouded by disappointment and by real or fancied neglect.

Macedonia was the next to adopt the plans of
Hannibal for a combination against Rome. The
new king, Perseus, restored to some extent the
prosperity of his own realm, gained the fickle
favor of the Greek cities, and conceived other alliances, which, however, were incomplete in 172 B.C.,
when Rome resolved upon war. For three years
the incompetent consuls accomplished little or
nothing; but in 168 B. C. Lucius Æmilius Paulus,
a patrician of the best sort, brought his energy and
ability to the conduct of the war. His legions
shattered the Macedonian phalanx at Pydna (168
B. C.), and with that battle broke the power which,
at the death of Alexander, a century and a half
earlier, had overshadowed all the East. The independence of Greece, Macedon, and Illyria was taken
away, and there was now no civilized court about
the Mediterranean in Europe, Asia, or Africa where
the authority of the Roman Senate was not recognized and obeyed. There were still semi-dependent
kings in Asia Minor and Egypt, but they only
awaited their doom. No monarch ventured to oppose his will to that of the Roman Senate.

Carthage was now a city of wealth and mercan-
tile prosperity. Her days of empire were ended,
but nothing could close her markets or her harbors.
Yet something of her old pride remained, and her
citizens were galled by the encroachments of Massinissa, whom Rome had established as king of
Numidia. Rome supported the Moor in his appro-
priations of Carthaginian territory and refused

either to send out an army or to allow Carthage to
protect herself.   Without troops, without a fleet,
without a leader, the desperate city took up arms
against the king, and the Senate, led by Marcus
Porcius Cato, interpreted this as an act of war
against Rome.   This third Punic war began in 149
B. C., with the Roman invasion of Africa.   Carthage yielded and was disarmed; but when the
Romans ordered the citizens to pull down their
walls and houses, and desert the old location for a
new site ten miles inland, the Phenician spirit
flamed out fiercely as it had done in the days of
Regulus.   The gates were closed against the
Romans, weapons were contrived in haste, a fleet
was built, and the defense maintained at terrible
sacrifice.   In 147 B. C. Publius Cornelius Scipio
Æmilianus, the son of Æmilius Paulus and the
adopted heir of the great Scipio, took charge of
the besiegers.   His lines cut Carthage off from
land communication and he choked the harbor
mouth with a wall of stone.   Pestilence and famine weakened the defenders, and in the spring of
146 B. C. the Romans scaled the ramparts.   The
citizens contested the possession of every house
and street, but fire and sword overcame them after
six days of bloody combat.   The walls and buildings were leveled and a curse was laid upon the
ashes of the city.   A part of its territory was
annexed to Numidia, Rome's subject kingdom,
and the remnant was made the province of
Africa, with Utica as its capital.   The name of

Carthage no longer existed on the maps of the world.

While Rome was wreaking this terrible vengeance upon Carthage the liberties of Greece and Macedon were expiring. After the fourth Macedonian war (148–146 B. C.) Macedonia became a province of Rome. The constant strife among the Greek States induced Rome to crush them into submission. Lucius Mummius defeated the Achæans at Leucopetra (146 B. C.), and in the same year obeyed the command of the Senate to destroy the city of Corinth, the metropolis of Grecian art, commerce, and civilization.

The Celtic tribes of northern Spain did not take kindly to Roman dominion, and the Lusitanians, dwelling in the region now known as Portugal, made serious inroads on the Roman provinces. Viriathus, the Lusitanian leader, was one of the ablest warriors that Rome ever encountered. With no advantages, except familiarity with the country in which he fought, this leader of half-civilized hordes held out for ten years (148–139 B. C.) against the best armies which could be sent to defeat him. The Roman governors were powerless to crush him and had recourse to perfidy. In 139 B. C. they procured his assassination, much to their relief, and soon brought his followers to terms. The Celtiberians in northern Spain were basely treated by the provincial prætors, and retaliated by a fierce war, in which they inflicted heavy losses before they had to yield.

To this same period belongs the Numantine War. Numantia, a town among the Spanish mountains, held out for four years single-handed against the Roman generals. The armies which had subdued the world could do nothing against these free people. The incompetence and faithlessness of the generals prolonged the war beyond all endurance. In 134 B. C., Scipio Æmilianus, who had commanded in the third Punic war, was sent to Spain. For many months the heroic Numantines withstood even his energy and determination. At last, worn out by their exertions, weakened by famine and disease, they set fire to their houses and died defiantly as the Romans broke into the town (133 B. C.).

These Spanish wars and the defense of Numantia are not to be ignored because of their small place in history ; they have a peculiar significance, and suggest important inquiries in regard to the condition of Rome at this time. The successful stands of Viriathus, of the Celtiberians, and of Numantia, are surprising, coming, as they do, at the time when Rome had shown herself incomparable in arms. The power which withstood the assaults of Hannibal was baffled by a tribe of savage mountaineers ! Carthage and Corinth, the " London " and the " Paris " of that age, were destroyed, but Rome met her match ten years later at Numantia ! It is true that a change had taken place at Rome. A transformation, outwardly for the better, but demoralizing within, was passing over the Commonwealth. It began at the close of

the second Punic war. The tribute money ex-
acted from Carthage and from the subject kingdoms of the East was the original agent of the
corruption.   The provinces which the Senate
erected from time to time out of its conquests
were ruled by Roman prætors, later by pro-
consuls, who took advantage of their brief terms
of office to plunder their territories. The taxes of
the provinces were farmed by Roman speculators,
who paid the State a round sum for the right to
collect the taxes and then extorted from the poor
provincials money enough to yield an enormous
profit. These tax-farmers were usually men of the
"equestrian order" (*equites*), and their subordinates in the provinces were the hated "publicans."
From the conquests in Greece and Asia the Romans gained new ideas of luxury which sorted ill
with their ancient simplicity. The art treasures
of Athens and Corinth were shipped to Rome to
adorn the city. The theater of Greece was copied
and the corrupt comedies were adapted to the
coarse language and ideas of Rome. The Greek
language, already the language of Roman books,
became the language of polite society. The sons
of rich men went to Athens to perfect their education, and Greek teachers established themselves
in Rome. The Romans began to spend more
money on their homes, on personal adornment,
and especially on their pleasures. It was an undoubted fact that the ancient strength of character which had been the pride of the race was

relaxing under the strain of foreign influence and increasing wealth.

Still another germ of disease in the State was slavery. This had existed from the most remote ages; but with the extension of foreign conquest it increased beyond all former limits. Slaves by the hundred thousand were imported from Greece and Asia, and every form of domestic and agricultural labor was wrested from freemen and imposed upon slaves. The cruelty of the Roman had not declined with the decay of his firmness, and the lot of the plantation-hand consequently had few ameliorations. It was a short life of utter misery. This slave-system was a two-edged sword cutting into the life of the republic: it maintained a population of several millions of men who were ready to seize the slightest opportunity to break away from their masters and begin the most terrible of insurrections, and it destroyed the dignity of free labor. The free agriculturists would not work with the chain-gangs, and the result was that the landless class in Italy, deprived of the means of support, flocked to the capital, forming a populace or rabble with which the government had to reckon at every turn.

Until this period of our history our information concerning Roman men of note has been so confused and so intermingled with fictitious tales that it has scarcely been worth the repetition. But from the era of the Punic wars until the last days of Rome there is a generally trustworthy record, increasing in copiousness with every decade and abounding in the names and exploits of individual Romans.

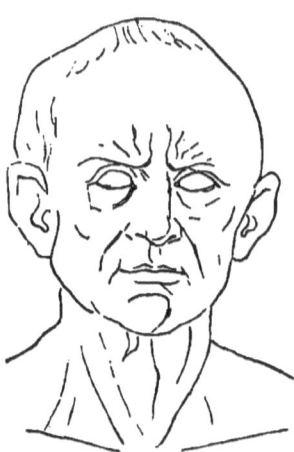

Marcus Porcius Cato and the two Scipios are the impressive figures in the epoch which we have just considered.

Cato, who is not to be mistaken for Cato "the younger" of a century later, was a type of the ancient Roman. He was born in 234 B. C., and lived a large part of his life in the country, where he

Marcus Porcius Cato.

owned and tilled a farm. From the rural assemblies and from service in the army he turned to Rome and engaged in politics as a reformer. His popularity, especially with the farmers, who flocked to the elections when he was a candidate, gained for him the highest offices in the city and important military commands.

Cato opposed himself to the flood of new ideas which swept in upon Italy after communication was opened with Greece. He revered the old Roman gods and respected the ancient Roman ideals of manliness, simplicity, and frugality. As censor his power was exerted to counteract extravagance and atheism and to strengthen the constitution on the old basis. As a statesman he saw the evils of the new *régime*, and sought to cure them by restoring the old. He had not the constructive ability to remodel the constitution to suit the altered needs of the State, and could only insist upon reviving its outgrown principles and combating what was firmly established.

Publius Cornelius Scipio was a man of other manners. His family, the Cornelii, were patricians of ancient lineage and boundless pride. The dark days of the war with Hannibal found the young Scipio distinguished among the city youth for his beauty, eloquence, and heroic conduct in his father's army. The dearth of great commanders at Rome, the failure of Hannibal's plan of conquest, and

Publius Cornelius Scipio Africanus.

the final resolve of Rome to end the war at any cost were his opportunity. By no means the equal of his opponent in genius, he defeated him at Zama and gained almost divine honors at Rome. After the wars in Africa and Asia, Scipio Africanus lived on a scale of luxury which called forth the condemnation of the stern old Cato and led to Scipio's withdrawal from Rome. He died in his voluntary exile about 185 B. C.

Scipio Æmilianus, the son of the brave Æmilius Paulus and the adopted heir of the great Scipio, was a worthy member of both families. As a soldier he won the title of " Africanus Minor " by the capture and destruction of Carthage, and of " Numanticus " by the reduction of the Spanish town. Into both these campaigns he entered with the old Roman energy, after his weakling prede-decessors had frittered away years and legions. His tastes were cultivated, and in Rome he sought out Greek teachers and studied the works of the Grecian sages. Æmilianus tried to stay the mis-fortunes which threatened the State ; but his talents as a statesman were exceeded by his good intentions, and bore but little fruit.

The outline of the second period of the republic has included nearly every country on the shore of the Mediterranean. The single Italian city which first achieved the supremacy of the peninsula has now become mistress of the world. In a third chapter we shall consider how the Roman system of government endured the enormous strain of this responsibility.

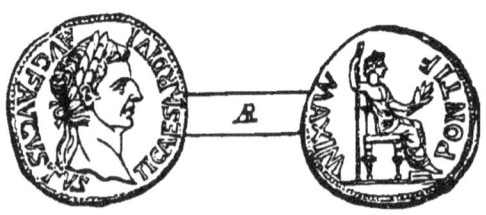

CHAPTER V.

SECOND PERIOD (Continued).

The Roman Republic.

Part III. (133–31 B. C.)

THE CIVIL WARS AND THE FALL OF THE REPUBLIC.

WITH the third and concluding period of the republic the history of Rome assumes a new phase. This period is the shortest, but it is crowded with memorable events; and remarkable men—among them two, at least, of the world's greatest—jostle each other on the crowded stage.

In considering the results of the extension of Roman dominion we were reminded of the evil influences which had thus been introduced into the once sober city. In the present division we must note the working out of these vicious principles in their many forms. We shall see their effect upon society and upon government both at home and in Rome's relations with foreign States; we shall examine the numerous attempts at reform and their successive failures, and we shall see how Julius Cæsar seized the crumbling constitution, arrested its fall, and, by instituting a strong central government under an absolute monarch, pre-

8

served for half a thousand years the vast empire which it had taken the republic half a thousand years to win.

War and conquest fill nearly every page of the record of Rome for the one hundred and fifty years between the passage of the Hortensian law and the outbreak of the land, or agrarian troubles, in the times of the Gracchi, 133 B. C. That famous law had opened every avenue of political distinction to the plebeians, and broken down the old social wall of patrician privilege. This led to a change in the office-holding class in the city. About the year 180 B. C. it was enacted that no man should hold one of the high (curule) magistracies who had not served ten years in the army. A minimum age was also fixed as a qualification for these positions. For aedile this was thirty-seven years, for praetor forty, for consul forty-three. It became customary also for the aedile to relieve the State of the burden of the expense of the national games and to bear it himself. This custom practically excluded poor men from the first step toward the consulship. Where it failed to exclude them it often did worse. Their political ambition led them to borrow the enormous sums which the aedile's display rendered necessary. This plunged the office-seeker into debt, out of which there was but one escape. The praetors and the consuls, at the expiration of their year of office, were assigned to the government of the provinces which were the spoils of foreign conquest. In the plunder of his province the debt-laden magistrate sought relief. The corruption of the provincial courts was incredible. The courts were controlled by the Roman governor, and too often his judgment was for sale to the highest bidder. Courts were established in Rome for the purpose of trying the persons accused of bribery and corruption, so extensive did these practices become; but the evil outstripped all the devices which were contrived to check it.

The Senate was largely recruited from the ex-consuls and ex-prætors, and thus became the repository of wealthy office-seekers and of needy and ambitious adventurers. The Assembly of the Centuries (Comitia Centuriata) which elected all high officers, had also suffered a change by which the first classes (see page 64) lost their right of influencing the election by casting the first vote. Men who owned no land were also enrolled among the centuries, so that this assembly became a democratic body in which wealth and family conveyed no special privilege.

The restrictions upon office-holding, together with the system of slave-labor and the changes in the comitia, caused a re-division of Roman society. There was the office-holding aristocracy, enormously wealthy or abysmally insolvent, and bent upon compelling a fortune out of the State. These men, mostly senators, gained the name of *optimates*, and they formed a body very difficult of access. A man who pushed his way to the

Senate by sheer force of talent as a general or orator was called a *novus homo* (new-man, fresh-man), and slighted and snubbed by his proud colleagues. The class of small farmers, who are the strength of any nation by reason of their intelligence, frugality, and conservatism, had disappeared from Roman society. The corn-kings and cattle-kings of the peninsula, with their boundless cattle-ranges and sheep-pastures, had crowded them to the wall. The slave system, importing its human victims by thousands and working them to an early death, destroyed the competition of free labor and left the Italian freeman no resource. Such as possessed the cherished rights of Roman citizenship sought the city, and, becoming tainted with the miasma of corruption which infected the official classes, made their citizenship yield them support. The offices of state were for sale to the man who should bid highest for the favor of the populace. The second class in the decaying republic were these people (*populares*), who exercised a political power which their character rendered dangerous. Demagogues instigated them against the optimates, and hurried them into projects of socialism and anarchy. Rich men courted their favor by open bribes, or by the more subtle method of distributing free bread and celebrating free festivals of costly grandeur. Between the populares and the optimates—the popular party and the senatorial party, as we shall hereafter call them—was a third party, or rather faction, whose weight was thrown on one side or the other of the scale, as its selfish interests dictated. This was the equestrian order (the *equites*, or knights of the Servian constitution). These men were capitalists from whom the senatorial party drew its recruits ; but the knights were not the social equals of the senators, and were made to feel their inferiority in a way which frequently drove them into popular alliance against the aristocracy. Besides these factions within the city there were thousands of men in Italy who had fought in the Roman wars and believed themselves worthy of citizenship. These Italians had a just claim to a share in the government, and Rome was forced to recognize it after a bitter war.

At the outset of the third period of the republic we have these elements of danger : A venal Senate, a distressed and discordant citizen-body, and a non-citizen population clamoring for recognition.

Two brothers, Tiberius Gracchus and Caius Gracchus, brought the civil strife to a head, and forfeited their lives by their efforts for reform. Tiberius Sempronius Gracchus, the elder brother, was but a young man when he entered public life. His ancestry was eminent. Cornelia, his mother, was the daughter of Publius Scipio, the conqueror of Hannibal, and her two boys, Tiberius and Caius, were the "jewels" which she had displayed to the boasting wife of a Roman millionaire. Scipio Æmilianus, his cousin and brother-in-law, was the leader of the aristocrats ; Appius Claudius,

his father-in-law, was a patrician of the best type;
but Tiberius, young, cultured, brave, and beloved,
cast his lot with the poor.

The tribunes of the people were established in
the first days of the republic to guard the infant
rights of the plebeians. With the equalization of
the orders the reason of their existence vanished,
but the office remained and tribunes were chosen
every year by the plebeian tribes. These officers
found a new field for action in the era of party
strife. They no longer served the interests of one
class, but utilized their high prerogatives as their
principles prompted or their interests paid. Thus
we shall see the tribunate divided against itself,
some serving the Senate, others obeying the populace. The tribune's power of veto and his influence in the assemblies made him the approved
instrument of political agitation, as we shall see.

Tiberius Gracchus was elected tribune of the
people at Rome for the year 133 B. C. and immediately proposed his measures of reform. The
young tribune—he was scarcely thirty—was versed
in law and history, and he knew that when, in
former times, Rome had been subject to similar
evils the tribune Licinius had passed a law which
had somewhat abated the misery. Rome was
overcrowded with idle citizens and Italy was in
the hands of a few landlords. The relief lay in
the re-division of the soil among the citizens.
That was the legislation of Licinius. This is
the Sempronian law of Gracchus : That all pub-

lic lands privately occupied should revert to the
State; that a commission of three men should de-
termine all questions of dispute concerning pro-
prietorship and should allow each occupier to retain from 500 to 1,000 *jugera* (300 to 600 acres),
and should distribute the rest of the recovered
public domain among the citizens and the Italian
allies, awarding homestead farms of eighteen
acres each to worthy applicants.   Such was Gracchus's great proposal.   It was wise and just, but
the way to its enactment was very hard, and its
enforcement was harder still.   The Senate, packed
with landed nobles, refused to entertain the proposition, and secured the aid of a tribune, Marcus
Octavius, to annul the acts of Tiberius.   The
latter destroyed the power of the former's veto by
persuading the people to depose Octavius from
the tribunate.   Such a thing had never been done
before, but the people obeyed their young champion and set aside the agent of the landlords.
The Sempronian law was passed, and its author,
with his father-in-law, Claudius, and his brother,
Caius Gracchus, were named as commissioners to
enforce it.   They encountered violent opposition
from the land-holders, and Tiberius, whose year
of office was expiring, feared the consequences in
case he should lose the protection of his official
title.   He seems to have been led astray by the
dangers of his position, and to have made high
bids for popularity and re-election.   The king of
Pergamon, in Asia, had lately bequeathed his king-

dom to Rome. The senators meant to administer
the estate to their own advantage, but Gracchus
asked the populace to vote the treasure for stock-
ing the farms of the new proprietors. Then he
asked their votes for a second term. The partisans of the Senate postponed the election and
raised the cry that Gracchus would be king. The
consul refused to suppress him, and a band of
young Roman lords rushed from the Senate-house,
struck down the tribune with their bludgeons, and
killed three hundred of his followers. (133 B. C.)
Here was the muttered thunder of an approaching
storm. Tiberius Gracchus fell the first martyr to
the contest of the classes. His cousin, Scipio
Æmilianus, followed him a few years later (129
B. C.), and his brother, Caius, ended a good fight
in the same tragic fashion in the year 121 B. C.

The vacancy in the land commission was filled
and the work of allotment went on for several
years as Tiberius had planned. The measure certainly afforded relief; but in 129 B. C. a dispute
with the Latin proprietors, on the ground of in-
fringement of title, brought the work to a close.
In that year Scipio Æmilianus, the hero of the
destruction of Carthage, was assassinated. He
was the leader of the senatorial party and a wise
and prudent statesman. Who murdered him was
never discovered, but his opposition to the Gracchan reforms had been bitter, and he was doubtless
removed for a political purpose.

The Senate tried to stop the progress of reform

by dispersing the reformers. The energetic pair, Caius Gracchus and Fulvius Flaccus, were sent out of the country, the former as quæstor in Sardinia, the latter as proconsul in that part of Gaul which is now known as southeastern France. The work of subjugation which Flaccus began was carried out a few years later, and the Spanish possessions were connected with Cisalpine Gaul by a new Roman province, Gallia Narbonensis, founded in 118 B. C.

In 123 B. C. Caius Gracchus left his province to take up his brother's work at Rome. He was a man of far greater genius than the martyred Tiberius, and his reforms looked beyond the relief of the poorer citizens to a genuine revision and reform of the political condition of the city. He was elected tribune of the people for 123 B. C., and re-elected for the succeeding year. The legislation of this brief period is a monument to his tremendous energy, resembling Cæsar's. Gracchus, like his brother, went to the people for his authority, and disregarded the Senate until he should accumulate sufficient power to break down that dignified assembly. He first won the friendship of the city rabble by a law providing that grain should be furnished to them by the State at a nominal price. This politic but unsound enactment allured thousands of indigent citizens to Rome, eager for bread and ready to support the leader who provided it without work. Having cemented his popularity with the masses by these largesses of grain, by re-asserting the Sempronian land-law, and by founding colonies in Italy and abroad, the reformer attacked the aristocracy. First he divided it, separating the land-holding senators from the capitalist knights (*equites*) by granting certain valuable privileges to the latter. Thus the knights were given the collection of the revenues of Asia and the jury duties and consequent fees at Rome. What the equestrian order gained the Senate lost; and the law-making power which the comitia was now exercising at the beck and nod of the tribune threatened that the Senate would be left behind in the development of the new constitution, as the Comitia of the Curies had been stranded long since.

But Gracchus overestimated his hold upon the populace. The Senate was aroused to protect its existence, and the tribune's proposal to extend full Roman citizenship to the Latins repelled the Romans themselves, more jealous than ever of their misused rights. The Senate put up a tribune, M. Livius Drusus, who promised the populace more favors than Gracchus had offered, and the fickle citizens deserted their old love for the new. In the elections for 121 B C. the popular tribune was defeated. His friends rallied to his defense on the Aventine Hill, but the optimates broke down their barricades. Caius, with a single slave, succeeded in crossing the Tiber, and in a grove on its farther shore their pursuers found the dead bodies of both. With the death of the Gracchi ended

a sincere effort for reform. The Senate saved itself at the expense of two patriotic lives and
much bloodshed. How well it deserved to live
and govern was shown by the events of the next
twenty years.

The war with Jugurtha (111–105 B. C.) is an
index of the sad condition into which the Roman
government had sunk. The following is the history of this wretched transaction:

By the terms of the second settlement with
Carthage, Rome assigned the rich African kingdom of Numidia to Massinissa, her ally in the second Punic war. His son, dying, left the kingdom
in common to his own two sons and his nephew,
Jugurtha, a brilliant young Moor who had served
in the Roman army at Numantia, and knew the
frail stuff which composed the nobility of the city
that ruled the world. Confident of his ability to
shield himself Jugurtha killed one of his royal
cousins and laid siege to the other, who straight-
way appealed to Rome for the protection which
the Senate owed. A senatorial commission came
to investigate, took Jugurtha's bribes, and gently
urged him to spare his cousin. The disrespectful
monarch sacked the town and slew Rome's royal
ward with cruel tortures. More than that, he slew
Roman citizens, and the tribune Memmius, in the
citizen assembly of Rome, called the Senate to
account for its scandalous perfidy. The Senate
declared war and sent a consular army to Africa,
but the generous Jugurtha sent the commanding

consul home a millionaire without a battle. Again
Memmius, the honest tribune, denounced the taker
of bribes, and the sluggish Senate summoned the
king to Rome for trial. But no one condemned.
The unpurchasable Memmius alone accused. The
other tribunes slunk away with heavy purses. Jugurtha was so confident of safety that he dared
to let loose his assassins upon a rival prince then
resident at Rome. This heinous murder was too
much. The Senate granted the popular demand
for war, and the king returned to Africa pronounc-
ing the famous judgment upon Rome: " O venal
city; thou, too, shalt perish when a purchaser shall
appear ! "

The second invasion of Africa failed as miser-
ably as the first. Jugurtha routed the consular
army, and sent it under the yoke of three spears
(*sub jugum*), which was the acme of disgrace.
The consul made a craven peace which the powers
at Rome would not ratify. Metellus, the able but
aged senator, who commanded the next expedition,
had two men in his army of whom the world was
to hear much—they were Caius Marius and Lucius
Cornelius Sulla. The latter was a young and hitherto reckless patrician of no reputation. The
former was forty-eight years old and a plebeian.
Marius was born on his father's little farm at
Arpinum, in 157 B. C. Some call him a day labor-
er's son. Out-door work hardened his constitution
to bear the strains to which his later life subjected
it. He joined the army, and served with credit

though without distinction. The popular party in the city made him tribune and afterward prætor. His faithfulness and his genuine interest in his soldiers and exertions in their behalf gained some recognition for him among military men, and doubtless led Metellus to select him as second in command. For two years the Romans accomplished little, and Marius accordingly conceived the idea of applying for the consulship and the chief command. Metellus scouted the possibility of his election, and advised him not to humiliate himself by going to Rome as a candidate. Marius not only went, but won. As consul (107 B. C.) he displaced Metellus, re-organized the army, enlisted soldiers from the city rabble, and drilled them to a perfection of discipline. These legions followed their horny-handed general now as they had not followed the perfumed senatorial chiefs. The really weak Jugurtha was easily crushed now that a man of honesty and energy opposed him. The ability of Sulla as quæstor under Marius hastened the end of the war (105 B. C.). Jugurtha was taken and brought to Rome, where he died in prison.

The military significance of the Jugurthine war was nothing, and the whole affair might be dismissed with a line of comment were it not for the exhibition which it furnishes of the utter weakness of the Roman Commonwealth. The wretched business of the earlier campaigns showed that the highest offices in the State were filled with bribe-takers. The successful candidacy of Marius

showed that a popular general might ride to the
highest place on the suffrage of the people.   Two
new characters, Marius and Sulla, have been introduced, and the praise which Sulla has won from
the Roman aristocracy for his part in Jugurtha's
capture has soured the temper of the jealous and
vindictive democratic leader.

During the African campaigns the Roman
armies in Europe were marching from one disaster
to another under the direction of incompetent
leaders.   Rome had no civilized enemy on the continent, but her soldiers found more than their
match in the half barbarous Germanic tribes which
were in turbulent commotion north and east of the
Alps, and from time to time sent hostile hordes
over the mountain barrier into the Italian plains.
In 113 B. C. the Cimbri defeated a consular army
on the north-eastern frontier, but turned aside to
Gaul (modern France) without pursuing their advantage.   In 109 B. C. and 107 B. C. the Roman
commanders in Gaul met the Cimbri and were repeatedly defeated.   In 105 B. C. these same barbarians destroyed two Roman armies on the lower
Rhone.   The citizens were panic-stricken.   Their
armies seemed useless, their generals incapable of
victory.   The Jugurthine war had just closed and
the populace assigned the command against the
Cimbri to their hero, Caius Marius.   A sudden
change in the movements of the barbarians granted
an interval for preparation.   In defiance of law
and custom Marius was made consul five times in

succession (104–100 B. C.). He made a few marked
changes in military organization and tactics, inspired his men with a share of his own confidence,
led them into Transalpine Gaul, and there, in 102
B. C., routed the Teutones in the renowned
slaughter of Aquæ Sextiæ. The Cimbri had
meanwhile swept around the Alps and entered the
valley of the Po, chasing before them the army of
Catulus, the patrician consul. Marius met them
at Vercellæ, broke their formation of battle, and,
aided by Catulus, inflicted such a blow upon them
that they abandoned forever their schemes of conquest.

The populace now had nothing too good for
Marius. Their hero had become their idol. He
was "the third Romulus," "the second Camillus."
His very boorishness of manner, which disgusted
the aristocrats, commended him to the democracy.
He had another element of strength—the veteran
army. The military reforms had altered the character of this force. It was no longer a national
guard of militiamen called from shop and plow
for a season and returning to their work at the
close of the campaign. The wide extent of the
realm and the attitude of the frontier tribes compelled the State to support a standing army of
regular soldiers—men whose only business was
war. The victories of Marius bound these reg-
ulars very closely to his fortunes. Henceforth the
leader of an army was a source of dread.

Marius, the soldier, was no statesman. He was

too honest to engage with all his heart in the wilder schemes of Glaucia and Saturninus, the leaders of the populace with whom he formed his first part-nership. These three men obtained the high offices for the year 100 B. C , and the tribune Saturninus revived the laws of Gracchus. New colonies were to be formed, and the public lands were to be assigned to the Ma-rian soldiers and the Italian allies. The promise of ra-tions at nominal rates se-cured the favor of the mob

Caius Marius.

of city voters. But the demagogues overreached themselves. The turbulence of their followers frightened the capitalists of the equestrian order, whom the Gracchan jury-laws had attached to the popular party, and even Marius wavered in their support. Saturninus and Glaucia grasped at illegal power, and the Senate commanded Marius, as con-sul, to protect the State. He obeyed, and a bloody battle was fought in the forum, December 10, 100 B. C. The senatorial party, led by the ex-chief of the people, triumphed, and the two popular leaders, together with many of their followers, were put to death. Marius was checked in his political career. The Senate had no further use for him, and the people hooted him in the streets. He left the city at the expiration of his sixth consulship, hating both citizens and aristocrats, but cherishing the dark prophecy that he should once more rule at Rome. "Seven times consul," an old witch had said.

Marcus Livius Drusus, "the Gracchus of the aristocracy," made a noble effort to cure the evils which preyed upon the State. He was a true aristocrat, and had the support of the best and ablest men of his order, but they were in a minority. His laws aimed to strengthen the Senate, to relieve the poorer citizens and the Italian allies. He proposed to transfer the jury-privilege from the knights to the senators, but to enroll three hundred new senators from the equestrian order. He would extend the distribution of grain, offer homesteads to the idle citizens, and finally raise the Italians to political equality with the Romans. The last proposition was the wisest of all, for Rome had already proved the incapacity of one city to rule an extended domain. But the jealous citizens charged Drusus with high treason. The dregs of the populace and the dregs of the Senate turned against him. An assassin struck him down (91 B. C.) and the Senate canceled his legislation.

Discontent with the failure of Drusus led the Italians to revolt. The Social war (war with the allies or *socii*) began in Picenum, in 90 B. C. The whole peninsula rose against Rome. Corfinium, under the new name Italica, was made the rebel capital of an Italian State. But the bonds

between the allies were loose and their organization poor. Rome pulled her forces together for
the struggle. By the Varian law the partisans of
Drusus were expelled from the Senate. A large
army was raised, and both Marius and Sulla offered
their services to the war department. Sulla was
given the leadership of the southern army and
Marius was assigned to the central division. To
break up the confederacy the Julian law (90 B. C.)
offered Roman citizenship to the Italians not yet in
revolt, and the Plautia-Papirian law, a few months
later, granted the same concession to all Italians
who should apply for it within sixty days. By
such seductions and by superior discipline the
dangerous insurrection was crushed (88 B. C.);
but it left a harvest of bitter fruits for the city.
The Senate had lost its ablest men by the Varian
law; the Italians were dissatisfied with the restrictions which were placed upon their newly-acquired
citizenship; Marius, the democratic general, and
Sulla, the aristocratic commander, were rivals and
enemies. At the same time the Senate declared
war against Mithridates, king of Pontus, who was
plundering and murdering Roman citizens in Asia
Minor. Sulla, with the army of the south, was
ordered to Asia to conduct operations against him.

To settle some of the harassing problems the
tribune Publius Sulpicius devised several laws.
The Senate was to be rehabilitated by the expulsion of its bankrupt members and the restoration
of the Varian exiles. The Italian citizens were to

have full political rights in the city. The Senate, led by Sulla, opposed the Sulpician reforms. Marius allied himself with the tribune, who persuaded the populace to transfer the conduct of the Mithridatic war from the champion of the Senate to the old friend of the people, the conqueror of the Cimbri. Sulla, at Brundisium, appealed to his soldiers ; they clamored to be led against Rome. Marius and Sulpicius could not collect a sufficient army to hold the city, and for the first time Rome was taken by Romans. Sulla forcibly quelled opposition, greatly increased the authority of the Senate, and after a few months in the city hurried to Asia Minor to prosecute the war.

Ever since the subjection of Antiochus the Great (189 B. C.) Asia Minor had been in a disturbed condition. Half a dozen discordant kingdoms, more or less under Roman influence, preyed upon each other. The distance of Rome itself and the corruptibility of the commissions of senators which were sent out to protect Roman interests gradually brought Rome into contempt. Mithridates, king of Pontus, despised her authority as heartily as did Jugurtha of Africa. This Mithridates was a remarkable man, of unusual stature, of surpassing bodily accomplishments, and of a tremendous mental and physical energy. The hard struggle which he gave the Romans led them to believe the current stories of his almost superhuman strength. They did not doubt that he had so inured himself to poisons that he was

safe from the usual terrors which haunted Eastern
sultans and was hardly able to take his own life.
Mithridates extended the boundaries of his ancestral kingdom, Pontus, on the Euxine or Black Sea,
until they included the eastern and northern shores
of that water. Having gathered wealth and power
• by these annexations he began a course of similar
encroachments on the west upon territories in which
Rome had an interest. Sulla, then governor of
Cilicia, forced the king to respect the decrees of
the Senate (92 B. C.). During the Social war in
Italy Mithridates repeated his aggressions so in-
sultingly that war—the first Mithridatic war—was
declared by Rome (89 B. C.). But the city had
scarcely troops enough to man her armies in Italy;
her allies were in revolt, and for a year the Pontic
king met no real opposition. He overran the
adjoining kingdoms and the Roman province of
Asia, proclaiming himself to Greeks and Asiatics
as a liberator. All the Italians in the province—
numbering at least 80,000—were murdered, without distinction, at his cruel command in a single day. Only a few small districts in Asia remained faithful to Rome, and without waiting to
reduce them the conquering army crossed the
Ægean to liberate Greece. The poor Greek cities,
constitutionally unable to stand alone, had already
suffered "liberation" at the mercy of Macedon
and Rome; but they were ready for more, and
Athens led the welcome to the invader.

We have now reached the point where Sulla,

having composed the affairs of the city and prop-
ped the Senate on its doubtful seat (see page 131),
took the field against Mithridates. With 30,000
men he crossed to Greece (87 B. C.) and drove the
invaders out of Athens and the Piræus. An over-
whelming army under Archelaus opposed him at
Chæronæa in Bœotia, but was beaten in an action
in which the aristocratic. commander exhibited
brilliant military genius.

Meanwhile there had been a democratic overturn at Rome, and the popular party had voted to
depose Sulla, and sent Flaccus, one of its own men,
to take his place. But it had become one thing to
vote the deposition of a successful commander and
quite another thing to compel him to give over his
army. Sulla gave no heed to the mandate of the
comitia; had no dealings with Flaccus, and continued his campaign against Mithridates, propos-
ing to finish with the business in hand and then
to settle in person with the unruly democrats at
Rome. Flaccus left Greece and crossed over to
Asia with the democratic army. Sulla inflicted a
second defeat on the Asiatics at Orchomenus in
85 B. C. and then led his devoted troops into Asia
by the land route. The civil war at Rome deluded
Mithridates into the belief that he could purchase
peace with one party by offering his aid to crush
the other. But Sulla was a hard man to hoodwink.
He guarded his own interests well, but he did not
neglect his duty. Mithridates signed a treaty with
him in 84 B. C. whereby the king agreed to give

up all his conquests and prisoners, to dismiss most of his army and navy, and to pay the expenses of the war. The revolted province of Asia was mulcted of a heavy fine ($24,000,000), and the few faithful towns were richly rewarded. The army of Flaccus now mutinied and joined the Sullan victors. The conqueror had finished the business in hand and now turned his hard face toward Rome.

There was need of him in Italy. He had left an optimate, Octavius, and a democrat, L. Cornelius Cinna, in the consulate at Rome. The latter was a firebrand. No sooner was Sulla in Greece than Cinna provoked a civil war (87 B. C.) by attempting to restore the canceled Sulpician laws (see page 130) and to recall the popular leaders whom Sulla had banished. The senatorial party broke up the comitia by violence and killed many of the multitude. For the safety of the State the Senate outlawed the democratic consul, but Cinna lingered in Italy and all the malcontents gathered about him. Marius, bowed with years, but still awaiting his promised consulship, hastened from his African retreat. The many outlaws of the Sullan revolution and the dissatisfied Italians helped to swell the democratic army. The rapid growth of the insurgent force created a panic at Rome. It was difficult for the Senate to raise a force and impossible to select a fit commander. Cinna cut off the sources of the grain supply and laid siege to the city. A pestilence within the walls helped his cause. Caius Marius, and Quintus Sertorius supplied the military genius which Cinna lacked. Their presence foreshadowed the result of a siege, and men from the garrison nightly deserted to the Marian camp. Without awaiting an attack the Senate surrendered, trusting Cinna's promises of mercy. Marius had promised nothing, and his will was stronger than Cinna's. He had been cast out by the city which once had hailed him as its saviour. The aristocrats had used him as their tool and thrown him aside in contempt. Their dragoons had hunted him out of Italy and harried his rest even in foreign lands. He was now seventy years old, ignorant as ever, still narrow in mind and changed only in the deepened intensity of his hate. At his command the soldiers disregarded the pledge of Cinna and slaughtered indiscriminately all the optimates who could be found. The list of the dead includes some famous names, but no noble name could slake the thirsty vengeance of the maddened Marius. The prophecy which had nourished his hopes during his later years was now fulfilled—at his order—and on the 1st of January, 86 B. C., he entered on his seventh consulship. One of his first acts was to give office to his nephew, Julius Cæsar, then sixteen years of age. Two weeks later he died in a raging delirium, furnishing in life and death an awful exhibition of the intensity of un-controlled revenge.

The democratic leaders triumphed in the blood of the aristocracy; but there was a specter left to haunt their dreams. Sulla, the greatest of the senators, was in Greece fighting for his country at the head of 30,000 devoted men. Flaccus, the successor of Marius, was sent to relieve him of his army and the conduct of the Mithridatic war (86 B. C.). How he fared in Greece and Asia we have already seen. Sulla went on with his campaigns as if his commission from the Senate had not been revoked. He was now legally an outlaw ; but an outlaw at the head of an army was a dangerous man to deal with. Still he was absent and fighting. There were the perils of war, of camp, and pestilence to take him off; perhaps he would never return. So, perhaps, Cinna reasoned for a time. It may be that he hugged the delusion the more closely as it showed signs of vanishing altogether. Year after year he made himself consul and ruled Rome as if there were to be no reckoning. His power was practically absolute. He was what no one would dare whisper that he was—a Roman king. The weakened Senate and the fawning rabble passed his laws. The Italians were accepted as genuine citizens of Rome, and the city mob drew its daily dole of grain from the government stores.

In 84 B. C. the outlaw Sulla wrote to the Senate. He had fulfilled his mission in Asia. Mithridates had acknowledged Roman supremacy and made amends for his misdemeanors. Sulla was now about to return, and he announced his intention of coming at the head of his army to restore the constitution as he had settled it in 88 B. C. At the news Cinna started to meet him with an army, but his soldiers mutinied and slew him (84 B. C.). The leadership fell to Carbo, the younger Marius, and Sertorius. Norbanus and Lucius Scipio were consuls for 83 B. C., the year in which Sulla landed at Brundisium with forty thousand men. Many senators came to his camp; one young knight, Cneius Pompeius (Pompey), led three legions of volunteers from Picenum and presented them to the delighted commander, who hailed him "Imperator." Sulla's aim was to gain possession of the capital and re-establish the rule of the Senate. He could not hope to reverse all the legislation of the democracy without estranging the allies, and he accordingly guaranteed to the Italians the fullest citizenship. The army of one consul he defeated, and that of the other deserted in a body to the Sullan camp (83 B. C.). The next year the armies of the government were more ably led, and the Samnites, always the hardiest of the allies, joined in the opposition to Sulla. But his generalship was unequaled among his opponents. His blows were sudden and heavy. With the odds against him he triumphed signally. The final battle was fought at the gates of Rome, in November, 82 B. C. Young Marius commanded his slaves to kill him; Sertorius escaped to Spain. For the third time the Romans had taken Rome.

Sulla's former capture of the city had been comparatively bloodless. Marius and Cinna had reddened the forum with aristocratic carnage in a vengeful frenzy, and Sulla's later acts eclipsed

even the Marian massacres in horror.   He was
not a man to be swept by passion, like the other
revolutionists ; revenge was not his inspiration,

neither did he covet absolute
power.   Himself an aristocrat
of the aristocrats, he believed
that his order was the only
one capable of governing the
State.   Of the common people
he feared nothing if left to
themselves.   It was when led
by the renegade nobles—the
Gracchi, the Cinnas, and the
like—that they were dangerous.

Lucius Cornelius Sulla. . He would, therefore, exterminate the moderate party in the Senate, the agi-
tators of the dull masses.   This was the policy
of the "Sullan proscriptions."   Lists were drawn
up of all the prominent men throughout Italy who
had sided with Cinna, sentences of exile or death
were pronounced against the proscribed, and their
property fell to the State and the informer.
Nearly five thousand names of "evil-minded"
citizens were listed, and most of them suffered
the execution of the sentence.   Their lands were
distributed among the soldiers of Sulla's army
and their slaves were made free citizens.

Sulla did not care for personal power; all his
measures were bent on giving the Senate monopo-
listic control of the State.   He doubled the number
of its members, gave them the jury-powers which

the knights had lately possessed, and abolished the power of the censors to expel senators. The tribunes were disqualified from holding any higher office, and in general the popular assemblies were deprived of authority. They could not even meet, except at the call of the Senate, and the Senate's sanction was indispensable to the validity of every law. With their political rights the populace also lost the free-grain grants which Gracchus had inaugurated. Sulla held the position of dictator for two years—a genuine king in power—and as soon as his "Cornelian reforms" were established withdrew to private life. He died in 78 B. C., in the full tide of his prosperity and in the enjoyment of the pleasures and successes for which he gave himself the title of Felix, "the Fortunate." His death left the Senate in control of the State, but, unfortunately, without self-control. Burdened with the responsibility of absolute power it staggered along to its destruction without guide or leader.

The task of preserving the Sullan constitution was difficult in itself—quite enough to occupy the attention of the Senate; but the problem was complicated by revolts abroad and insurrections at home.

At Sulla's death the consul, Marcus Lepidus, a member of the popular party, made an effort to overthrow the recent reforms. But the other consul, Catulus, backed by the Senate, the survivors of Sulla's army, and the troops of Pompeius,

crushed this movement (78-77 B. C.). The soldiers of Lepidus who escaped made their way to
Spain, where the democratic cause had a stout
champion.

Sertorius, an exile from Italy, founded an independent kingdom among the Lusitanian mountains
in Spain, and for eight years (80-72 B. C.) success-
fully resisted the senatorial armies, led by such
men as Metellus and Pompeius. A jealous lieutenant murdered him (72 B. C.), and was himself
defeated and put to death by Pompeius. While
Pompeius was in Spain a dangerous outbreak oc-
curred in Italy. At Capua was a school where
athletic slaves were trained for the sword-fights
which were a popular feature of the public games.
One of these gladiators, Spartacus, a Thracian, inspired his fellows, mostly his countrymen and Gaulish prisoners of war, to kill their guards and escape.
Their plan succeeded, and the liberated bandits in-
fested the sleeping crater of Vesuvius and robbed
all the country round. Other gladiators followed
their bold example. Slaves crowded to them from
the neighboring barracks. Spartacus defeated the
bands which Rome sent against him and felt
strong enough to fight his way out of Italy. But
his subordinates were unruly, and the temptation
of rich spoils kept them in the peninsula, which
they ravaged, like Hannibal, unchastised for two
years (73-72 B. C.). In 71 B. C. the prætor,
Marcus Crassus, scattered the slave army, and with
the assistance of Pompeius, just returned from

Spain, put an end to this disgraceful Servile war. A pack of half-armed slaves had roamed through Italy for three years. Surely the reformed Senate was no more capable than in the days of Jugurtha!

Pompeius and Crassus received the consulship as a reward for ridding the State of Sertorius and Spartacus. They signalized their year of office (70 B. C.) by forming an alliance with the popular party to cut away several of the newly-set props of the Senate. The tribunes were reinstated in their old privileges; the jury duties were divided between the senators and knights, and the power of removing senators for cause was restored to the censors. Thus the chief clauses in the Sullan constitution were canceled by two men who had fought in his army, but who now took sides with the common people. The grain largesses had already been restored, so that the city rabble peaceably regained nearly all that it had lost in the aristocratic revolution.

It was the absence of strong government in Italy which allowed the Servile war to grow to dangerous proportions, and it was the same weakness abroad which allowed the pirate power to flourish in the Mediterranean and Mithridates to re-commence his aggressions upon the provinces and allied kingdoms of Rome in Asia Minor.

The second Mithridatic war (83–81 B. C.) made no change in the terms of peace as Sulla had arranged them in 84 B. C.; but in 74 B. C. a third contest opened between the Senate and the ambitious king. Tigranes, the son-in-law of Mithridates, was now King of Armenia and the most powerful ruler in Western Asia. He refused his aid to Mithridates, but Sertorius, in Spain, and the pirates who swarmed in all the seas lent valuable assistance. Lucius Lucullus led the Roman army in eight campaigns (74–67 B. C.). He fought on sea and land, captured numerous fleets, and destroyed powerful armaments. In 73 B. C. Mithridates fled to the court of Tigranes, whither Lucullus followed him. The veterans won the famous battle of Tigranocerta, 69 B. C., and then crossed the Euphrates in pursuit of the kings. Here the army mutinied, and clamored to be led home (68 B. C.). The people at Rome had authorized the discharge of the veterans, and there was no alternative for Lucullus but to abandon his advantage and leave the two kings unconquered. In 66 B. C. Pompeius superseded him in the command.

While Lucullus had been performing wonders among the deserts and mountains of Asia another set of generals had been marring their fortunes in the war with the pirates. These buccaneers had regular organized governments, with fortified harbors and strong castles, and no part of the Mediterranean was free from their depredations. Their fleets levied contributions from isolated towns, seized the Roman grain and treasure-ships, captured travelers and held them for ransom. In Crete and Cilicia their strongholds were especially numerous. In 78 B. C. their audacity aroused the wrath of the Roman Senate, and throughout the next ten years expeditions were sent against the pirates. Cilicia was wrested from them in 75 B. C. and Crete in 68 B. C. Although two of their nesting-places were broken up the foul brood was not destroyed. There was need of a more comprehensive plan and more energetic action. In 67 B. C. the Gabinian law clothed Pompeius with unlimited power over the waters of the Mediterrranean and its coasts for fifty miles inland. Whatever he wanted of money, ships, or men, he had full warrant to take, and he was given three years for preparation and execution. It was a decree of the people, not a law of the Senate, which conferred this unprecedented royal authority. Pompeius acted rapidly, and within three months swept the pirate power from the seas. On the strength of this brilliant exploit the tribune Manilius proposed Pompeius as the man to take up the war against Mithridates, which had languished since Lucullus was recalled. The "Manilian law" was passed, and Pompeius thus added the full command of Asia to his pro-consular power over the seas and coasts. He was already on the ground, and received from the reluctant Lucullus the travel-worn legions. In 65 and 64 B. C. he drove Mithridates from Pontus and conquered Tigranes. The new Roman possessions were assigned to vassal kings. Mithridates's spirit broke at last, and he killed himself (63 B. C.). Pompeius took Jerusalem and set up Roman authority there (63 B. C.), and lingered

in the East several years longer before returning
to Rome for his triumph (61 B. C.).

While Pompey, the general of the Senate and
the leading Roman, remained in the East, the city
itself was the scene of a deep laid and well nigh
successful conspiracy to overthrow the Government. By some unexplained circumstance the
plot to make Crassus dictator, with Julius Cæsar
his lieutenant, for the year 65 B. C., failed. In 64
B. C. a new conspiracy was hatched. This time such
great men as Crassus and Cæsar kept aloof from
the plotting, or at least acknowledged no connection with it. The leadership was left to an entirely
different set of men. Foremost among them was
Lucius Sergius Catilina (Catiline), a patrician and
a senator whose ability was as marked as his
profligacy. Catiline was well qualified for his dangerous work. He had the boldness and the wickedness of a hardened criminal, and was so deeply
in debt that only robbery could extricate him.
His followers were a motley set. "Outcasts from
honor, fugitives from debt, gamblers and ruffians,"
said Cicero. These men had no higher aim than
plunder, but many believed that behind this an-
archistic screen the real leaders of the democracy,
even Cæsar himself, were concealed. Catiline
had the audacity to stand for the consulship for
the year 63 B. C., but he was rejected, and a new
man (*novus homo*) gained the coveted office. This
man was the Roman Demosthenes, Marcus Tullius
Cicero.

Cicero had come to the city in his youth from his home at Arpinum, the birthplace also of Caius Marius. Weak of body, but strong of mind, his ambition kept him out of the usual military paths to honor and office and directed him to the arduous way to the Senate-house which led through the forum and the law-courts. Cicero was neither rich nor favored by influential friends, but his intellect and his billiant oratory conquered the difficulties of public life. Keeping generally on the side of the Senate in the strife of parties, Cicero made his way through the various grades of office until, in this conspiracy-year, 63 B. C., he was consul. The senatorial party were inclined to sneer at this countryman of no ancestry who had pushed his way among them, and the sensitive and conceited orator suffered intensely from their coldness toward him.

Marcus Tullius Cicero.

In 63 B. C. Catiline's plans were matured. He would stand for the consulship, kill his competitors, summon the nondescript army which he had collected in Etruria under his friend Manlius, and give over the city to fire and plunder. By the agency of a woman the consul Cicero discovered the plot, and on November 8, B. C. 63, laid his information before the Senate. Catiline, the impersonation of audacity, sat in his place among

10

the senators and listened to Cicero's famous har-
rangue beginning : " How long, O Catiline, wilt
thou abuse our patience ? " The arch-conspirator
fled from the city, leaving trusted agents to kill
Cicero, fire the city, and open the gates to him as
he should return with Manlius's army. These
agents bargained for an alliance with the envoys
of the Allobroges, a Celtic tribe. But Cicero's
men captured the envoys as they were leaving
Rome and found upon them treasonable letters to
the Celtic chiefs. The conspirators in the city
were also arrested. The papers were opened and
read in the Senate. There was no longer any
doubt of their guilt. The question arose as to
what should be done with the conspirators. Cicero
refused to decide, and laid the matter before the
Senate. Some favored death, others imprisonment.
Capital punishment was unusual at Rome, and could
not legally be inflicted except after trial by due
form of law and by the sanction of the citizens.
But the danger was pressing; Catiline was marching on the city; the whole State seemed to be un-
dermined and ready to explode. Cæsar voted no,
but Cato—the younger of that name—turned the
tide. He denounced the milder senators as part-
ners in the crime. There was a hurried change of
votes, and the Senate decreed the immediate execution of the prisoners. They were strangled in
prison a few hours after. Cicero flattered himself
that his consulship had saved the State. Cato
hailed him *pater patriæ,* " father of his country,"

and he retired from office steeped in glory, as his extant letters testify. The "army" of Catiline and Manlius was defeated at Pistoria (62 B. C.) and the renowned Catilinarian conspiracy was thus brought to an end by the death of its leader.

CHAPTER VI.

SECOND PERIOD (Continued).

THE ROMAN REPUBLIC.

Part III (Continued). (61–31 B. C.)

FROM THE CONSPIRACY OF CATILINE TO THE FALL
OF THE REPUBLIC.

CRASSUS, Pompeius, and Cæsar have already
figured in this history and will become still more
prominent. Their respective characters and political connections must be thoroughly understood in
order to the comprehension of the history of the
closing years of the republic.

Marcus Licinius Crassus was the type of the
Roman knight. His family was good, but not of
the highest rank, and his ability was mainly in the
line of money-getting. The vast extent of Roman
possessions afforded a wide field for a man of such
conspicuous business talent as Crassus possessed.
He was the Rothschild of his time; a banker with
nations for his clients, a contractor upon public
works—in short, a bold and successful manipulator
of capital. He had some military talent, and had
put down the Servile war. He had much polit--
ical ambition, and had been consul with Pompeius

in 70 B. C.   The consuls of that year had signalized their term by an alliance with the popular party to do away with the Sullan legislation.   In this way Crassus had lost caste with the Senate, without being fully adopted as a leader of the democracy.

Cncius Pompeius was also of the knights.   His family were outside the sacred pale of the aristocracy, and his father had been thought lukewarm in his support of the Senate.   Pompeius was born in 106 B. C., and was reared as a soldier.   We saw him at the age of twenty-three levying volunteers for Sulla, and so gaining the dictator's approbation.   That leader sent him to quench the democratic fires in the Sicilian and African provinces (80 B. C.), and on his return allowed him,

Cneius Pompeius
Magnus.
Pompey the Great.

young as he was, the honors of a formal triumph, and the title of Magnus—"the Great."   As the general of the Senate Pompeius ended the Sertorian war in Spain, and was in at the death with Crassus when the gladiators of Spartacus were captured.   With Crassus, too, as consul (70 B. C.) he had helped the knights and democrats to strip the Senate of its privileges.   He gained rich rewards from the people by the Gabinian and Manilian laws (67, 66 B. C.), which intrusted the entire military strength of the realm to him for

three years. He cleared the sea of pirates and
Asia of enemies. All parties were afraid of him,
and had he combined his soldierly qualities with
statesmanship he might have mastered the government as another ambitious general did twenty
years afterward. But Pompey had lived too long
in camps. He had little facility in dealing with
the populace or the politicians, and he had no
oratory to sway the Senate. He thought the grate-
ful nation should grant him all his requests out of
thankfulness for his victories, and he sulked at
home when his demands were denied. He was
" out " with the Senate, which feared him, and no
longer " in " with the democracy, which had now
in Cæsar a more sagacious leader.

   Caius Julius Cæsar, the head of the popular
party, was born in Rome, July 12, 102 B. C.
(otherwise stated 100 B. C.), of
excellent patrician family. The
Julian *gens* had numbered many
consuls and prætors in its list of
honors, but this baby boy was destined to eclipse them all. Cæsar's
aunt, Julia, married Marius, the
rough democratic soldier, and just
before he died the " seven times
consul " honored his nephew by

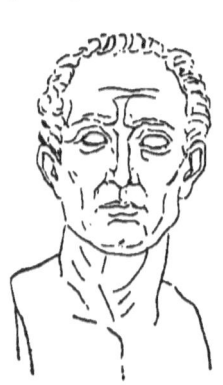
Caius Julius Cæsar.

appointing him a *flamen dialis*, a
high-salaried officer under the State religion. Young
Cæsar married the daughter of the consul Cinna,
and showed his mettle by defying Sulla's com-

mand to divorce her. He was outlawed, but escaped death in the proscription—perhaps, from his obscurity, for he had displayed little ability in his subordinate military service in Asia. Pardoned after Sulla's death, he served as quæstor in Spain (67 B. C.), and sank his fortune under a load of debt by the magnificence of his administration as ædile at Rome (65 B. C.). In 63 B. C. the people elected him *pontifex maximus*, the head of the religious order, in spite of the fiercest senatorial opposition.

He was the only great man in Rome. Pompeius and Crassus, at the head of their legions or their loans, were rendered prominent by circumstances; but Cæsar alone saw exactly the weakness of the State and a way to set it right. He formed a purpose and arranged his plans for its execution. His purpose was to put an end to the murderous strife of parties by crushing both in his own mailed hand. But as yet the hand held no weapon of offense. To carry out his plan an army more loyal to himself than to the State was a necessity. To secure such a command for himself Cæsar joined the First Triumvirate (60 B. C.).

Rome had become accustomed to civil strife, and the return of Pompeius from the East was awaited with alarm. But the conqueror came back as a private citizen, merely asking the Senate to ratify his acts in Asia, to reward his soldiers, and grant him the honor of a triumph. The demands were not too great, but the Senate, fearful of raising any man to eminence, refused to grant them. The politic Cæsar, who had lately returned from Spain much improved in fortune, showed himself a friend to the slighted general, married his relative Pompeia for a third wife, and interested both Pompeius and Crassus in an arrangement for the benefit of all three. By this private bargain—the First Triumvirate—the three magnates divided the offices among themselves. Cæsar's share was one year of consulship (59 B. C.) and five years as governor of Gaul. This was his chance to pay his debts and train an army. Pompeius was to have what the Senate had refused him—a triumph, the ratification of his Asiatic policy, and lands for his soldiers. Crassus took nothing, but secured certain privileges for his order, the knights. In his consulship Cæsar fulfilled his promises to Pompey, the Senate, led by Marcus Porcius Cato, an old-fashioned aristocrat, vainly opposing. In 58 B. C. he went to his province, which included Gaul on both sides of the Alps. Pompeius remained in Italy to watch over the distribution of lands among his disbanded veterans. To cripple the Senate, the democracy, led by Publius Clodius, sent Cato to the East on a public mission, and banished Cicero from Italy for killing the Catilinarian conspirators without trial.

The details of Cæsar's Gallic wars are not to be followed here; it is enough to say that in eight years he subdued the Celtic tribes living in the countries now known as France, Belgium, and the

Netherlands, crossed the Rhine and chastised the
Germans, crossed the Channel and commenced the

conquest of Britain. His campaigns left Gaul
thoroughly pacified and partially Romanized ; the
Latin language took hold of its people, and it rap-

idly assumed an important place in the empire. In this warfare Cæsar developed the rarest military traits. He was prompt, energetic, fertile in resource, and careful of his men. He bound the army to him by kindness, by liberality, and by complete mastery of his profession as a soldier.

While Cæsar the politician was in Gaul, making a new reputation as Cæsar the general, Pompeius was doing police duty at Rome—watching the parties and endeavoring to shape a course between the factions. Clodius, the demagogue, was outbidden by the demagogue Milo, who persuaded the populace to recall Cicero. Cato's term expired, and he, too, came back to Rome (57 B. C.). The consequent increased prestige of the Senate led the triumvirs Pompey and Crassus to meet Cæsar at Luca in his province, 56 B. C., to arrange a new programme. Cæsar stipulated for the extension of his term for another five years. At its close he was to be consul for 48 B. C., and was to be excused from coming to Rome as a candidate. Pompey and Crassus were to be consuls (55 B. C.), followed by five years of pro-consular government, the former in Spain, the latter in Syria. The terms of the bargain were carried out. Cæsar went on with his conquests; Crassus went to Syria, where he was killed after the Parthians had defeated him in the great battle of Carrhæ. Pompeius sent lieutenants to manage his Spanish province, but himself lingered at Rome.

The death of Crassus destroyed the triumvirate.

Cæsar's daughter, Pompey's wife, died.   The Senate feared Cæsar's return more than the greatness of Pompeius.   The disorders in the city warranted the Senate in proclaiming martial law.   Pompeius was ordered to enforce the measure; he accepted the commission, thus becoming the open defender of the aristocracy and the consequent foe of Cæsar's friends, the democrats.   The breach between Cæsar and the Senate was openly made and widened rapidly.   Cæsar was safe while in Gaul at the head of an army; but under the laws he could not return to the city without resigning his command.   The law which made him pro-consul had declared that he might be a candidate for the consulship for 48 B. C. without complying with the usual formality of presenting himself in person to the city electors.   The Senate insisted that this law was invalid, and that Cæsar must resign if he sought office before his term of command in Gaul expired.   In the excited state of the city at that time he would certainly have been imprisoned upon his return, even had he escaped assassination. Throughout the years 51 and 50 B. C. Cæsar and the Senate fought a battle of diplomacy on this point.   Cæsar was absent, to be sure, but he had become wealthy in Gaul and could buy the support of consuls and tribunes as he needed it.   His creature, the tribune Curio, accepted the Senate's bill deposing Cæsar, but demanded that Pompey should lay down his power at the same time.   Pompeius refused.   The struggle, which was nominally be-

tween the Senate and Cæsar, became actually a
duel for the supremacy which must end in the monarchy either of Cæsar or Pompey. The latter
assumed command of the army in Italy in December, 50 B. C., at the request of the consuls-elect.
On January 1, 49 B. C., a final letter from Cæsar
was read in the Senate. While maintaining the
justice of his position, he offered to give up the
greater part of his provinces and all but one of
his legions if he might stand for the consulship
in his absence. But the Senate, which had pinned
its faith upon the generalship of Pompeius, declared
Cæsar a traitor if he should not immediately resign
all his command. Curio and Antony hastened to
him at Ravenna with the news. It was expected.
The Senate had declared war, and there was no
time to lose. "The die is cast," said Cæsar, as he
led his army across the little river Rubicon which
divided his province from his country.

In the Civil War there is nothing more remarkable than the consummate military genius exhibited by Cæsar. Pompey the Great was a soldier
of more than ordinary talents. But his reputation
had outstripped his merits. The fame of his
early achievements under Sulla, his share in the
Sertorian and Servile wars, his suppression of
piracy, and final victory over Mithridates and the
East, constituted an unbroken series of successes
whose marked contrast with the sorry failures of
most senatorial generals, made him seem to the
aristocracy—and, doubtless, to himself—invincible.

Cæsar, on the contrary, had left Rome eight years before with no military record. He was now a conqueror, but surely, reasoned the nobles, it was not so hard for a Roman to subdue the half-barbarian Gauls and Germans. It would be a different matter to make head against Cneius Pompeius Magnus! So they thronged to the head-quarters of the Pompeian army in Campania confident of victory, and eager for the battle which should put an end to Cæsar's presumption. But Pompeius was too cautious to oppose Cæsar with a small or an undisciplined army. While he awaited recruits at Capua Cæsar was in vigorous action. His veteran legions were hurried into Italy, the young men of Cisalpine Gaul, to whom he had promised Roman citizenship, poured into his camps and overtook him on the march. He waited for nothing, but hastened down the eastern side of the peninsula, sending Marcus Antonius (Mark Antony) over the Apennines with a detachment to take the road to Rome. Pompeius lingered at Capua and did nothing. He expected the Italians to enlist under him, but there was scarcely an Italian town on Cæsar's route that did not welcome the democratic leader. Not only the Italian citizens, but the Roman garrisons in their citadels hailed the conqueror of Gaul as a friend. Domitius Ahenobarbus occupied a road-fortress and attempted to block the path of invasion. His troops mutinied and gave him up to Cæsar, who pardoned him and his companions. Pompeius waited no longer. In April, 49 B. C., he crossed from Brundisium to Greece with his army and a cumbrous crowd of senators and aristocrats, abandoning Italy without a battle. Henceforth Italy was Cæsar's, but the empire was not yet won. The Pompeians held Spain and Africa in the West and the entire Roman dominion in the East. Greece was a convenient recruiting-ground, and from his station there Pompeius could gather strength until fit occasion offered to recross the narrow seas and give battle to the usurper.

Cæsar did not follow; he had no fleet, and he was confident that Pompeius would not soon feel strong enough to attempt the re-conquest of Italy. Rome was without defenders and Cæsar entered the city unopposed. If the aristocrats had feared what the massacres of Marius and Sulla gave them reason to expect they were pleasantly disappointed. Life and private property were spared. The remnant of the Senate declined to grant Cæsar's request for the consulship, and he accordingly assumed the responsibility of government. With the authority of the popular assembly he drew money from the public treasury and hastened to Spain to crush the Pompeian party there. Before the end of the year he completed the work and returned to Rome. The people named him dictator, but he resigned this office and was chosen consul for 48 B. C., the office which had been promised him at the meeting of the triumvirs at Luca in 56 B. C., and from which the aristocrats had endeavored to exclude him. The Senate was now in Greece with Pompeius, holding sessions and formally conducting the Government.

Cæsar stayed but eleven days in Rome, and then hastened to Brundisium, to forestall, if possible, Pompey's return. The latter had a great army of Romans and allies, and a numerous co-operating fleet. By his own good fortune, or by the stupidity of the commander of the senatorial fleet, Cæsar with half his force crossed the sea unopposed. The other half, under Mark Antony, was cooped up at Brundisium. The Pompeian army was encamped at Dyrrachium. Cæsar had landed south of that point. Antony ran the blockade and landed further north. The two armies united before Pompeius was aware of their temporary isolation. But he broke through their lines and marched into Thessaly in the spring of 48 B. C. This slight success convinced his party that the next battle would be Cæsar's ruin. The next battle was fought at Pharsalus, August 9, 48 B. C. The Pompeians were utterly routed. Thousands were killed, and twenty-four thousand surrendered to Cæsar and his twenty-two thousand. Pompeius fled to the sea-shore and took ship. On landing in Egypt he was murdered by order of the king. His lieutenants dispersed throughout the provinces, fearful of Cæsar's vengeance.

It was the conqueror's purpose not to build until he had laid the foundation. The Romans heaped their honors upon him—the consulship for five years, the tribunate for life, the dictatorship for one year; but he did not return to the city while enemies remained in the provinces. Egypt was his first destination. Here the rise of the Alexandrines and the Roman garrison placed him in extreme peril, from which he was saved by courage and promptitude. With timely re-enforcements he defeated the Egyptian army. Cleopatra was established as queen, and then Cæsar hurried off to Asia Minor. Pharnaces, the son of Mithridates, had extended his dominions, thinking to go unnoticed and unpunished in the tumult of the Civil war; the pro-consul had opposed him in vain. Leaving Alexandria, Cæsar hurried through Syria and Asia Minor to Pontus, demanded the submission of Pharnaces, and compelled it after a five days' campaign. "*Veni, vidi, vici,*" "I came, I saw, I conquered," is the famous form in which he announced his victory.

The East and most of the West were now at Cæsar's feet. His mastery of the Roman world was assured, although the two sons of Pompeius, with Cato and other irreconcilables, hopelessly defied him in Africa and elsewhere. Cicero had cut a poor figure in the affairs of the past two years. By nature and training a conservative, he had clung to the senatorial party, though he did not abandon Italy with its leaders. After the death of Pompeius he accepted Cæsar's government as an established fact, and was thereupon read out of the senatorial party. Still he took no earnest part in public affairs, and was regarded as a political trimmer whose course was determined by his personal safety rather than by principle. The men who had the most to fear from Cæsar—Labienus, his old lieutenant, Sextus and Cneius Pompey, Afranius, and Petreius—and the fanatical adherents of the lost republican cause, like Cato, collected a formidable army at Utica, near the ruins of Carthage, in Africa. On his return from the East by way of Italy, Cæsar had to face a new peril. His successes thus far had been won by the fidelity of the legions which he had trained in the Gallic wars. They had sympathized with his cause and had shared his campaigns. They now demanded rewards and release from service. The tenth legion, which had borne the brunt of the hardest attacks in Gaul, broke into open mutiny and appealed to Cæsar to redress their wrongs. He satisfied them, and by a wonderful display of coolness and tact won them back to renewed devotion. Losing little time at Rome, Cæsar crossed to Africa (47 B. C.) and routed the republican army on the field of Thapsus. His soldiers, wearied with chasing rebellion around the Mediterranean, granted no mercy; 50,000 men were killed; Cato, "the last of the Romans," died a republican, falling on his own sword rather than

Marcus Porcius Cato.
"Uticensis."

11

accept pardon from Cæsar. Labienus and the
sons of Pompey rallied a new army in Spain, but
Cæsar, who had already neglected Italy too long,
returned to Rome (46 B. C.). There he celebrated
four magnificent triumphs—for Gaul, Egypt, Pontus, and Africa—and delighted the populace with
splendid shows and games.

Cæsar was really king or emperor of Rome.
The Senate—what was left of it after the Civil
war—and the public assemblies existed only to
give formal assent to his decrees. He wore the
purple robe of royalty, but the old prejudice
against kings denied him the title and crown.
Yet he was made dictator for ten years, and then
became censor and high-priest for life. Uniting
these offices in himself he set about his reforms.
These measures were not intended to revive the
old constitution. In the struggles of the hundred
years' war the Gracchi had tried to save the State
by magnifying the power of the popular assemblies, and Sulla had strengthened the Senate with
the same end in view. Cæsar allowed both Senate
and assemblies to exist, but deprived them of real
power. All responsible authority centered in himself as monarch of the Roman Empire. Candi-
dates for public office, like the laws, must have his
approval. In the army, the legislature, and the
Church, he was supreme. The ancient republican
forms, Senate, comitia, consuls, prætors, and tribunes, remained, but their life was extinguished.
From the chief executive power in the State the

Senate was degraded to the place of an advisatory council. Its membership was raised to nine hundred, and its aristocratic exclusiveness was invaded by the admission of prominent men not only from the Italian cities but from Gaul and Spain. Besides these foreigners even some of the liberated slaves were admitted to seats in this old chamber of the nobles. The Cisalpine Gauls were confirmed in the rights of citizenship which Cæsar had promised them. The great body of Roman law was reduced to systematic form and published to guide the decisions of the law courts. Even the calendar was reached in this comprehensive scheme of reform, and the Julian solar year of three hundred and sixty-five days and six hours superseded the irregular year of twelve lunar months, by which time had hitherto been computed.

In the midst of these plans of re-organization Cæsar was called to Spain by the defeat of his lieutenants. He took with him Octavianus Cæsar, his grand-nephew and adopted heir. The Pompeians offered battle on the plain of Munda, near Cordova, March 17, 45 B. C. They knew the temper of Cæsar's soldiers and understood that defeat meant death. The two armies were of nearly equal strength, and both were ably led. There was no skirmishing, no exhibition of tactics; the men fought fiercely at close range with sword and spear, their leaders in the thickest of the fight. Cæsar's desperate efforts and his personal bravery won the victory. Thirty thousand Pompeians, including many of rank, fell, but Sextus Pompey escaped to the mountains. Munda was the imperator's last great battle; after restoring his authority in Spain he returned to Rome.

Measures for the consolidation and defense of the empire occupied the great man's mind. The provinces had hitherto suffered from the loose government of the Senate; Cæsar took to himself the right of appointing the provincial governors. Criminals had escaped through the right of appeal to an easily-influenced populace; Cæsar abolished the right of appeal except to himself as supreme judge. Short terms of office and frequent changes had diminished the authority of the magistrates, and enhanced the power of the perpetual Senate; Cæsar held office for life and gained the right to name his successor. Other generals had made conquests and organized provinces without regard to the interests of the empire; Cæsar endeavored to form a "scientific" and easily-defended frontier. The Rhine, the Alps, the Danube, the Caucasus, the Euphrates, were the natural boundaries of the empire, and he recognized the folly of gaining a precarious foot-hold beyond them. At one important point the frontier of Rome was still weak, and the dignity of the Roman arms was not respected. It was on the borders of Syria, where the Parthians had defeated Crassus, the triumvir (53 B. C.). Cæsar meant to avenge that insult, and made preparations for a Parthian campaign. A republican conspiracy prevented their completion.

Cæsar had pardoned his enemies, but they had not forgiven him. The aristocrats who had escaped alive from the Civil war were not proscribed. The dictator treated them with kindness and forbearance, gave them honors, seats in the Senate, and provinces abroad. But his effort to attach them to his person was a failure. The remnant of the ancient aristocracy, whose incapacity to govern had brought on the evils that Cæsarism was trying to correct, still plotted in secret for the old constitution. Cicero was, in heart, at least, with this republican faction, though his voice was on the side of Cæsar. The leading conspirators— nearly all senators of high birth—were M. Junius Brutus, Cassius, Decimus Brutus, Trebonius, Cimber, and Dolabella. Marcus Junius Brutus deserves especial mention. He was the nephew and son-in-law of Cato, the sturdy patriot who had killed himself at Utica rather than survive the republic. Brutus shared his uncle's devotion to the republican form of government; he was honest, and held a high place in the esteem of Cæsar and of the Senate. But the conspirators persuaded him that Rome was suffering from another tyranny like that of the Tarquins,

Marcus Junius Brutus.

and that, as in the ancient days, a Brutus must bring back the republic. It was easy to work upon his sentimental and superstitious tempe-ament, and he was soon won over, notwithstanding the tokens of Cæsar's confidence which he had received.

Many features of the dictatorship aroused the Roman prejudice against kings. Cæsar's purple robe and golden chair, his concentrated power, and his selection of his own successor, were sufficient evidence of the royal character of his position; still he put away the offered crown. As the Ides of March (March 15, 44 B. C.) drew near preparations for his assassination were perfected. Sixty senators were implicated in the plot, and rumors of their purpose were not silent in the city. Cæsar was warned, but took no precautions and provided no body-guard. As he entered the meeting-place of the Senate on the morning of the fatal 15th the "liberators" crowded upon him and attacked him with their daggers. Pierced with twenty-three wounds he fell and died at the foot of a statue of Pompeius, which stood by. Brutus, the fanatic, dipped his blade in Cæsar's streaming blood and brandished it in the face of Cicero, crying, "Liberty is restored!"

But liberty was not restored, as the liberators themselves learned. Mark Antony was consul and an executor of Cæsar's will. He made alliance with Lepidus, Cæsar's lieutenant, who was at the gates with an army. Veterans of the Gallic wars, who cared more for their former leader's memory than they did for the republic which he had overthrown, were in the city awaiting the lands which had been promised them. Antony, Lepidus, and the army had not entered into the conspirators' calculations, and their sudden appearance altered the footing. Instead of treating Cæsar as a traitor the liberators humored the temper of soldiery and populace by granting his body honorable sepulture. The remains were placed in the forum, and there Mark Antony addressed the people. He read the dead man's will, which bequeathed his money to each citizen and his gardens to all. Gaining their favor thus he played upon their feelings, showed them that it was as their champion that Cæsar had risen and triumphed, and as their friend that the aristocrats had struck him down. He inspired them with frenzied devotion to Cæsar and fierce hatred of

Marcus Antonius.
" Mark Antony."

the conspirators. In solemn enthusiasm they built a funeral pyre in the forum, and there burned the body of their dead hero.

The conspirators, alarmed by the popular horror at their deed, dispersed in haste. To several of them provinces had been assigned by Cæsar. Marcus Brutus was to govern Macedonia, and Decimus Brutus was to have Cisalpine Gaul. Antony had fully determined to succeed to Cæsar's power, and had no mind to allow these two neighboring and wealthy provinces to remain in the hands of the leading conspirators. He accordingly persuaded the people that the late dictator had changed his intention regarding the appointments. Marcus and Decimus Brutus were, therefore, assigned by popular decree to other offices, and the government of both Macedonia and Cisalpine Gaul was given to Antony himself. But the governors had already reached their provinces and must be expelled. Decimus Brutus, in northern Italy, was the first to be attacked. While Antony was in the field against him the young Octavius returned to Rome from Greece, accompanied by his friend, Agrippa. The adopted son and heir of Cæsar was in his nineteenth year. The news of his uncle's death and his own preference in the will aroused his ambition, and he hastened to Italy, taking the adoptive name Caius Julius Cæsar Octavianus. With the adroitness of an older politician he ingratiated himself with Cicero and the Senate, posing as the friend of the republic and the foe of Antony. Cæsar's old soldiers hailed with pleasure the handsome youth whom they had seen in Cæsar's company. He had certainly some elements of strength, and the Senate was in sore need of a champion. Cicero's keenness had penetrated the purposes of Antony, against whom the great orator

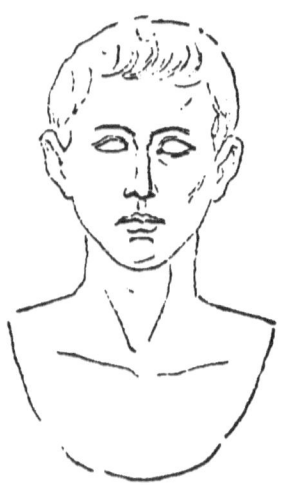

Cæsar Octavianus.
"The Young Augustus."

was now thundering his Philippics. By his marvelous eloquence he aroused the Senate to action.
The boy Octavianus was given a prætorship and
a military command, and sent northward with the
two consuls of 43 B. C. to crush Antony, who was
declared an outlaw. Both consuls perished in the
war, and the heir of Cæsar was thus left at the
head of an army. The Senate had intended to
throw him over as soon as he had served its purpose, and now refused him the consulship which
he demanded. He, too, crossed the Rubicon and,
contrary to the Senate's express command, entered
the city and compelled the assembly to elect him
consul. This chief magistrate, aged twenty-one,
secured a decree of outlawry upon Cæsar's assassins and then returned to the north. Lepidus,
Cæsar's former "master of the horse," and Antony, joined their forces and routed Decimus Brutus. Octavianus threw over the Senate's cause
as the Senate would have abandoned him. With
his uncle's friends, Antony and Lepidus, he formed
the Second Triumvirate (43 B. C.) "for establishing the republic." For the present there was to
be no division of power among the three generals.
They were to have equal consular authority for
five years, and their acts were to be beyond the
jurisdiction of Senate or assembly. The "republic" which they established was really the Cæsarian government, with a tripartite dictatorship.
Such a government was destined to last only until
dissensions should reduce the triune dictatorship

to a monarchy. In Italy the triumvirs had equal authority; Spain and the West were assigned to Lepidus, Antony took Gaul, on both sides of the Alps; Africa, Sicily, and Sardinia fell to Octavianus. The East was prudently reserved for later division, as it was already in the hands of the conspirators. Brutus was in Macedonia, assembling the troops which Cassius and others had collected in Asia. This republican army was formidable in numbers and composition, and really threatened the discomfiture of the triumvirs. Before assuming charge of their provinces the latter resolved to attack Brutus. Previous to leaving Italy, however, they secured a formal vote of the people legalizing their actions, and then in cold blood set about the proscription of their private and political enemies. The lists of the proscribed included hundreds of honorable citizens who were the victims of personal spite or of the informer's greed. The patriotic Cicero, whose vanity and political indecision do not invalidate his claim to the second place in the Roman honor-roll, was murdered to gratify the hate of Antony (Dec. 7, 43 B. C.).

The republican army numbered 100,000 men, gathered from all the Roman East. Extortion and plunder supplied the funds for its support. In 42 B. C. Antony and Octavianus passed over to Epirus with a force of equal if not greater strength. The heirs of Cæsar and his murderers met at Philippi, in Thrace, afterward famous as the

home of the first Christian church in Europe.
Two battles were fought here in November, 42
B. C. On the first day Cassius was defeated by
Antony and killed himself in despair, ignorant
that the division of Octavianus had meanwhile
been driven back by Brutus. The death of Cassius deprived the republican army of its real leader.
Brutus was a philosopher, but no ruler of men,
and his soldiers broke loose from all restraint.
Twenty days after the first battle a second was
fought. The result was doubtful, and Brutus,
despairing of success and deserted by his legions,
took his own life. The triumvirs conquered, and
the last struggle for the old republic was at an
end.

Lepidus, rich and indolent, had been neglected
in the late campaign, and was slighted in the
re-distribution of the prov-
inces, receiving only "Africa,"—that is, the small
Roman province of that
name. Already the theo-
retical equality of the triumvirs was disturbed, and
the two naturally stronger
men were asserting their
authority. From Philippi
Antony marched through

Cleopatra.

Asia, reclaiming the East. In Syria he met the
far-famed "Serpent of the Nile," Cleopatra, the
woman whose beauty had captivated Julius Cæsar

and won for her the throne of Egypt. The rough triumvir was an easy conquest. He accompanied her to Alexandria, her capital, and lived there with her in the most shameless and extravagant debauchery. His wife, Fulvia, and his brother, Lucius Antonius, were in Italy, and stirred up a civil war in the hope of summoning him to Rome. They thwarted the efforts of Octavianus to regulate affairs at home and to reward his soldiers by grants of land and the foundation of new colonies. In conjunction with Lepidus he

Marcus Æmilius
Lepidus.

took up arms against the Antonians and captured their stronghold, Perusia (41 B. C.). These disorders recalled the pleasure-loving Antony to his senses. He hurried to Italy with an army, and there came to an understanding with his colleagues. Lepidus was content to retain the administration of his single province, while Octavianus took the West, with Italy, and Antony the East, with Cleopatra. The marriage of Antony and Octavia, young Cæsar's sister, sealed the bond of reunion. This partition of the Roman lands did not convey the sovereignty of the sea. Sextus, that vigorous son of Pompey the Great who had escaped death at Pharsalus, Thapsus, and Munda, had gathered a fleet and placed himself at the head of the Mediterranean pirates. He did not care to renew the battle for the republic, but he had his father's death to avenge and his family fortune to recover. Rome's food supply came from Sicily, Asia, and Africa by sea, and the ships of Sextus, by the capture of the grain-fleet, held the city in constant peril of famine. To buy him off, the triumvirs, in 39 B. C., signed the treaty of Misenum, in which they agreed to restore his father's confiscated millions and allow him full control of Sicily, Sardinia, and a large part of Greece. But Sextus offended Octavianus by seizing an Italian coast town, and the triumvirs soon re-opened the war. In 37 B. C. the Sextian fleet was soundly beaten and its pirate admiral deprived of power. Lepidus asked that Sicily be now added to his department; but the western ruler, jealous of his territory, not only refused this favor, but took Africa for himself, thus thrusting Lepidus out of the triumvirate (36 B. C.). In 38 B. C. the term of the three men had been extended for a second five years, and Octavianus and Antony had thus three years more of power. The former adopted the policy of Cæsar and undertook campaigns against the Illyrians, who intervened between the Roman province and the River Danube, the natural boundary of conquest in that direction. In his military and naval operations the triumvir, still under thirty, had the advice of Marcus Vipsanius Agrippa, and in all business of civil government the knight, Cilnius Mæcenas, was his trusted counselor. In the East Antony held royal court at Alexandria. The

Egyptian, Cleopatra, was favored, and Octavia, his proud Roman wife, was put aside. His expedition against the Parthians, 36 B. C., was an utter failure; but a later raid into Armenia yielded the honor of a triumph which, to the disgust of the Romans, was celebrated in Alexandria instead of at Rome. This report fed the current suspicion in Italy that Cleopatra had persuaded Antony to discrown the queen city of the world and remove the capital of the Roman world to Alexandria. Antony's treatment of Octavia widened the breach between the triumvirs. In 32 B. C. the smoldering rivalry burst into the flame of war. Antony and Cleopatra collected an enormous armament for the invasion of Italy. Four Asiatic kings contributed to the army, and the ships of many nations composed the fleet. The delay consequent upon the assemblage, transportation, and sustenance of such a force enabled Octavianus and his lieutenants to summon the utmost of his comparatively meager resources. The East was populous, wealthy, and full of ships and seamen. The West was inferior in all these particulars, but immeasurably superior in the personality of its present leader. Antony was broken by dissipation, infatuated with a wicked woman, and could not command the confidence of his motley army. Octavianus Cæsar had the advantages of a great name, of ten years' honest and capable administration, of a united and devoted following, and of Agrippa's constant counsel and encouragement.

The two armies confronted each other for a time in Greece. Desertions from Antony's army alarmed him. On the 2d of September, 31 B. C., the two fleets engaged in a naval battle. After the first encounter Cleopatra turned her vessel's prow toward Egypt. Antony saw the movement, joined her on board, and the craven pair deserted the sea-fight, which became a scene of rout and destruction. Octavianus was completely victorious, thanks to the skill of Agrippa. The Antonian army surrendered as soon as the fate of the fleet was known.

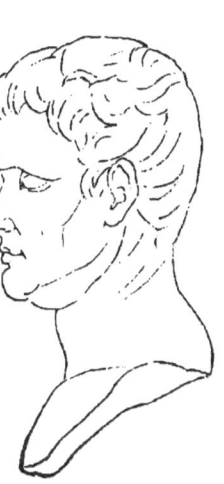

Marcus Vipsanius Agrippa.

The next year (30 B. C.) the victor invaded Egypt. Antony's resistance was but half-hearted, and his troops refused to fight. Even Cleopatra, foreseeing his ruin, and bent on making good terms with the new master, turned from the lover whom she had dragged to ruin. When her servants falsely told him of her death, Mark Antony, the friend of Cæsar and the ruler of the East, destroyed his miserable life. Alexandria surrendered to Octavianus, but the conqueror did not bend the knee to the city's queen. She had hoped to take captivity captive as she had done before; but the new Cæsar was forewarned of her wiles. He spared her life to grace his triumph at Rome, but she escaped that humiliation. In some unknown way, perhaps by

the sting of an asp, as some of the old stories have
it, her spirit followed the ruined Antony out of
the world in which it had so delighted.

The deposition of Lepidus and the death of
Antonius reduced the triumvirate to its lowest
terms. The power which this board of three men
had usurped in the confusion after Cæsar's death
was now concentrated in the single survivor,
Octavianus. Julius Cæsar had forever answered
in the negative the question whether the republic
could longer exist. The hundred years of civil
war from Gracchus to Cæsar had proved the incapacity of the Senate as a governing body, and
the reformers, the Gracchi, Drusus, Sulla, had suc-
cessively failed to create a competent and stable
government out of either of the elements at hand,
the aristocracy or the democracy. A king was
inevitable, and years of proscription and civil
murders taught the Romans the folly of resistance. What the republic could do it had already
done. So long as its citizen-body and its aristocratic Senate were simple, sober, frugal, and patriotic, its power extended. The citizen armies of
Rome conquered Italy, Carthage, the western and
the eastern world. But wealth and power brought
to the aristocrats decay of morals, greed of power
and gain. The slave system destroyed free labor
and exterminated the middle class of citizens.
With a corrupt nobility and a beggared populace
the State lost its balance. The provinces were
misgoverned and robbed ; successful generals

seized the civil power. At last a general and a statesman crushed the whole frail fabric of the republic and made himself monarch of the Roman world. He fell a victim to the sentimental attachment which a few still cherished for the old Commonwealth, but the republic never got upon its feet again; after a dozen years of divided sovereignty Cæsarian power was reunited in the person of Cæsar Octavianus, the very person whom the great founder of the empire had chosen to succeed him. Thus the worn-out republic expired, and a greater monarchy took its place, a little less than five centuries after the last Tarquin king was banished by the first Brutus and the patrician revolution.

When the first monarchy closed Rome was supreme among the Latins, the farmers who tilled the soil of Latium; the new monarchy found Rome the capital of the world.

Coin of Antony and Cleopatra.

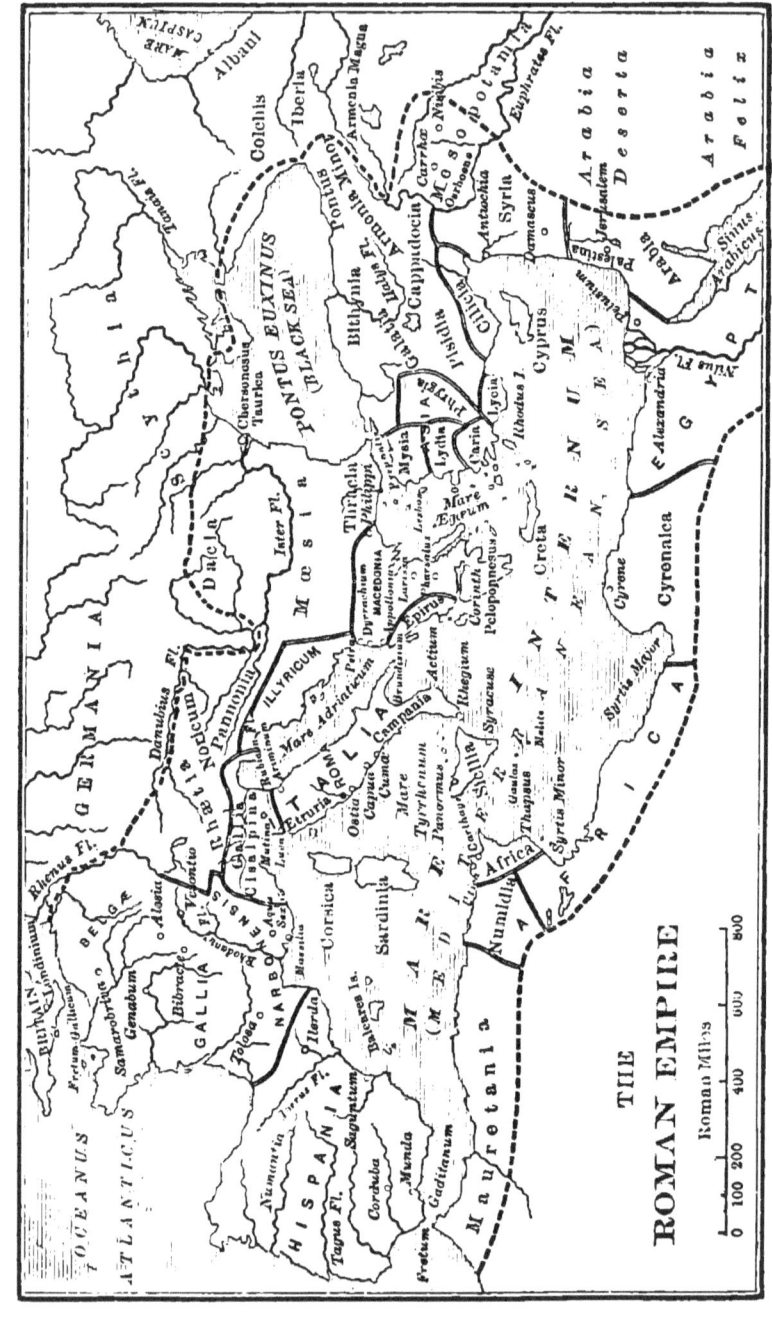

THE

ROMAN EMPIRE

Roman Miles

0   100   200   400   600   800

CHAPTER VII.

THIRD PERIOD.

The Roman Empire. (507 years.) 31 B. C.–476 A. D.

Part I. 31 B. C.–192 A. D.

FROM AUGUSTUS TO COMMODUS.

The defeat of Antony, B. C. 31, left Cæsar Octavianus sole master of the many lands which the Roman republic had conquered. After years of foreign war and civil strife the world was at peace. The doors of the Roman temple of Janus, which were always open in war-time, were now closed for the third time in history—once before, in the reign of Numa Pompilius, and again after the second Punic war. Having crushed all opposition in the East Octavianus returned to Rome (29 B. C.) to celebrate his triumph and to organize a system of government for the vast empire of which he was the undisputed chief.

In this work he enjoyed the able assistance of Agrippa and Mæcenas, and profited by the warning example of Julius Cæsar, who, confronted by a similar task, had called down his own destruction by too bold assumption of royal prerogatives and symbols. There are several reasons for the success of Octavianus in a task in which his greater kinsman, Julius, failed. The very fact that there had already been a Cæsar detracted somewhat from the popular dread of an absolute ruler. During the protracted civil wars a generation had grown up which had no personal knowledge of the better days of the republic, and consequently preferred peace and material prosperity under the new *régime* to a renewal of war and sacrifice for the re-establishment of the Commonwealth. Moreover the new government assumed the form and donned the outer garb of the old. We shall see how the old republican institutions faded by scarcely visible degrees into the new empire.

Octavianus assumed neither the symbols nor the

title of king. "Imperator" was a term already in use to designate an officer who held a high military command. As commander-in-chief of the army Octavianus and his successors bore that title, to which our ears are accustomed in its shortened form "emperor." The emperor was also elected to all the high offices of the republic. He was

Augustus. First Emperor. (31 B. C.-14 A.D.)

dictator, with the supreme authority which always accompanied that position; as consul he could convene the Senate; as censor he could enroll or expel members of that body; as tribune he was the special magistrate of the common people and his life was sacred; the State religion was under his care as pontifex maximus. A new title was needed to comprehend all this authority, and accordingly in 27 B. C. the Senate decreed to Octavianus the surname of Augustus ("his majesty"). This name was assumed as a title by all his successors, but to Octavianus, the first who bore it, it belongs in an especial sense, and henceforth Augustus is his name. The sixth month of the Roman year was named Augustilis (August) in his honor, as the fifth had been named July, from his father Julius.

It had been a fruitful source of Roman ills that the republican Senate had applied no coherent system to the government of the outlying provinces. To hold a nation by force of arms while a prætor or proconsul plundered its treasury was the Senate's highest achievement in provincial government. The consequence had been a constant tendency in the realm to fall apart. The Augustan system was an undoubted improvement. Augustus classed the provinces as senatorial or imperial. The former, being thoroughly subdued and far from the frontier, were administered by governors appointed by the Senate as heretofore, except that a financial agent accompanied them to collect the emperor's private share of the revenue. The "imperial" provinces were those of more recent origin or more exposed situation. These were administered by the legates or military lieutenants of the imperator.

This resulted in a uniform method of control. So long as the emperor was vigilant in his superintendence of his legates, and was himself honest and just, the provincials were well governed. As the empire became more firmly established they were encouraged to aspire to the full rights of Roman citizenship, which had already been extended to Latins, Italians, and Cisalpine Gauls. When this process of Romanization was completed the provincials considered themselves no longer as vanquished people, but as fellow-countrymen of the Romans and partakers in Roman greatness. Gauls, Spaniards, Greeks, Asiatics, Africans, and Egyptians were proud of the Roman name and "the eternal city," now for the first time really their capital.

Augustus strove to make Rome worthy of the empire. The buildings of the city were shabby, the streets narrow and steep, the public squares and temples small and unkept. The epoch of civil disorder had wasted the money which should have gone for public works. Hundreds of buildings were now pulled down at the emperor's order, new squares were laid out, fine houses erected, temples renovated, and walls repaired. A police force preserved order in the city and throughout Italy, then, as now, a favorite haunt of brigands. The splendid roads which radiated from Rome through the peninsula were extended to all parts of the empire, and a postal system for the use of the government facilitated rapid communication with distant provinces. The age was one of material prosperity. Peace and better government nurtured commercial activity. Trade sprang up between the provinces, lifting to wealth and prominence many happily-situated ports about the Mediterranean. It was the boast of Augustus that he "found Rome built of brick and left it built of marble;" but his reign left something more enduring than the finest product of the Parian quarries. His friend Mæcenas was the especial patron of art and letters, and his encouragement and bounty made Rome for the first time in its history a literary center. In the sunshine of imperial favor flourished the poets Virgil (70–19 B. C.), Horace (65–8 B. C.), Tibullus (54–19 B. C.), Propertius (49–15 B. C.), Ovid (45 B. C.–17 A. D.), and the historian Livy (59 B. C.–17 A. D.).

The wars of Augustus were chiefly along the frontiers of the empire. Scarcely a province revolted from its allegiance, and the government was thus left free to regulate its boundaries. Roman dominion was extended to the Danube (29–15 B. C.), the free remnant of Spain was subdued (27–19 B. C.), and the Parthians, who had not yet been chastised for their insult to the Roman arms at Carrhæ, voluntarily returned the trophies of that victory and made peace. Gaul, the field of Cæsar's exploits, was in full process of Romanization as far as the Rhine. But the Germans who dwelt in the unknown forest region beyond the river were a constant menace to the peace of the em-

pire.   On the Rhenish frontier, accordingly, the
Roman armies were concentrated, and frequent raids were made across the stream, not so much for purposes of conquest as to deter the Germans from invading Gaul.   These campaigns were conducted by Drusus and Tiberius, the sons of Livia, whom Augustus had married, and whom the Senate honored with the title of Augusta.   Drusus died in Germany, but his brother estab-

Livia Augusta.

lished Roman authority in portions of Germany and Pannonia (Hungary), after a fierce struggle in which the Roman legions were often worsted and Italy itself panic-stricken with fear of invasion.

The later wars of Augustus were conducted almost wholly by his lieutenants.   His active life had begun at an early age, and his responsibilities weighed heavily upon his rather sickly constitution.   The last years of his life were clouded with trouble.   The marvelous good fortune of his public life was awfully compensated by family ills. The emperor had no sons to succeed him.   Drusus, the best of his step-sons, was dead.   His daughter and granddaughter disgraced his name by their wickedness and were banished.   His grandsons, Caius and Lucius, died in young manhood, leaving him only an idiot heir.   It was whispered at Rome that Augusta was concerned in these untimely deaths, and was exercising more than motherly solicitude for her own son, Tiberius, who lived now a prince at Rome, now a gentleman at Rhodes, now a general in the German camps, growing old in the uncertainty whether he or another should succeed Augustus. The emperor's domestic ills bred melancholy, which was deepened by a calamity which befell the State. In the year 9 B. C. Quintilius Varus, with three legions, was defeated in the Teutoburger Forest, in Germany, by a chief, Arminius, or Hermann, who has become the national hero of the Germans. Varus was killed and his army massacred by the Germans, smarting from Roman aggression. Rome shuddered at the news. Again, as in the times of Brennus, Hannibal, the Cimbri and Teutones, the storm had come out of the north. Though past his seventieth year, weak in body and disturbed in mind, the emperor prepared to punish the revolted Germans. But death came upon him before the task was done. He died peacefully at Nola, near Naples, in his seventy-sixth year, having been sole ruler of the civilized world for forty-four years (31 B. C.–14 A. D.).

During his life Augustus was considered something more than a mortal. The decay of the ancient religions of Rome and Greece had left men's minds in a strange and expectant attitude toward supernatural things. Some looked for a return of the old Saturnian times—the primitive golden age ; the Jews looked for a Messiah. In the East first, and afterward in western lands, there arose a strange veneration of the emperor.   When he died the Senate publicly proclaimed him a god (*divus*), and shrines were built throughout the empire for his worship.   At Ancyra, a town of the Galatians, was such a temple.   On its walls was chiseled in Greek and Latin, for the world to read, the story of Augustus as he wrote it out himself.   Not many years ago this record was re-discovered and published to the world.   The emperor sets forth plainly and proudly the events of his reign, ignoring one, the greatest.   For in Bethlehem, an obscure village of his dominions, in the twenty-seventh year of his reign, the Lord Jesus Christ was born.

There was no law to regulate the succession to the throne which Augustus had established so

quietly that the Romans still thought and spoke of the republic as if it were yet in existence.   As an adopted son Tiberius was, however, the emperor's legal heir. The main army was in Germany, under Tiberius's nephew, Germanicus, and at the news from Rome the soldiers urged their leader to claim the throne for himself.

Tiberius. Second Emperor
(14–37 A. D.).

He modestly declined in favor of Tiberius.   The Senate bestowed upon the latter the same offices

which his step-father had held. He too became
Cæsar, Augustus, imperator, pontifex maximus,
tribune, etc., and was indeed a monarch under
republican disguise. Parts of the outgrown republican apparel were now discarded. The Comitia lost its dignity, and its rights of electing magistrates and approving laws were transferred to the
Senate. But the Senate gained little by the transfer, for it dared reject neither the laws nor the
nominees of the emperor. The ruler's power was
further increased by means of the laws against
treason and by the organization of the Prætorian
Guard. The laws placed it in the power of the
sovereign to exile any person proved to be dangerous to the State, the State being interpreted to
mean the ruler. Informers (*delatores*) were paid
to ferret out and accuse such political criminals,
and the most trivial offenses were made the ground
for action. The Prætorian Guard was a picked
body of 6,000 men who were established in a permanent camp just beyond the city wall. They
were practically the garrison of the city, and
later, as their numbers were increased, they, as
the only armed force near the capital, set up
and pulled down emperors themselves. This institution was an outgrowth of the later years of
Augustus.

Augusta, the empress-mother, shared the chief
power with her son until her death (29 A. D.), and
seems to have been the abler ruler of the two.
Under their joint direction Germanicus defeated

Arminius the German, thereby gaining such favor with populace and soldiers that the government thought best to send him to Syria on a dangerous expedition, from which he never returned. Tiberius was past middle life at the death of Augustus, and age came rapidly upon him. After nine years of capable administration he allowed his favorite courtier, Sejanus, the commander of the prætorians, to govern for him. In 27 A. D. Tiberius withdrew from Rome to the Island of Capri, near Naples, where he wasted his life in disgraceful dissipation, while his favorite ruled the empire in his name. A rival brought news to Capri that Sejanus was plotting to displace his master and proclaim himself emperor. At the command of Tiberius the favorite was seized and executed, and another minion, Macro, installed in his stead. The miserable existence of Tiberius was terminated in

Caligula. Third Emperor (37-41 A. D.).

37 A. D. by death. He, too, was given divine honors by the servile Senate. It was under a magistrate of Tiberius, Pontius Pilate, governor of Judæa, that Jesus Christ was crucified (30 A. D.) for proclaiming himself King of the Jews.

Tiberius appointed Germanicus's son Caius and his own grandson as joint heirs of his property and power. But Caius had the

favor of the prætorians and of the people, and the
Senate could only ratify their choice. Caius
Cæsar Germanicus is known to history as Caligula
("Bootkins"), the name by which his father's soldiers called him when, as the baby of the legion,
he toddled about the camps in his soldier-suit.
He was a willful and weak-headed tyrant, vexing
the State with extravagant and insane undertak-
ings, and corrupting society by his gross immoralities. He claimed to be a god, and required worship of his subjects; he built a bridge of boats
across a bay that he might "walk upon the
waters;" he led his legions to the "conquest of
the ocean," bidding them gather
sea-shells as spoils of victory.
After bearing with his mad
whims for four years two of his
officers stabbed him to death in
a theater (41 A. D.).

Caligula was a young man at
his death, and left no heir. The
Senate seized the opportunity to
re-assert its own supremacy, and
undertook to conduct the government without an emperor.

Claudius. Fourth Em-
peror (41–51 A. D.).

But the Senate reckoned without the new element
—that Prætorian Guard which Augustus and Tiberius had formed for the support of the ruler.
The prætorians found Caligula's uncle, Tiberius
Claudius Nero, hiding in the palace, dragged him
to the camp, and hailed him as imperator. The

Senate yielded, not daring to oppose the only
armed force in Italy. During his nephew's lifetime this Claudius, who was deformed in body and
of unsound mind, was the sport of the emperor
and his court. The Emperor Claudius had but
little to do with the actual business of the government, his low-born favorites in the palace exerting
a controlling influence upon all his acts. Pallas,
his steward, and Narcissus, his secretary, were the
real authors of his policy, and they used their influence to enrich themselves by the shameless sale
of offices and privileges. Felix, who trembled before his prisoner, St. Paul, was another of Claudius's wicked parasites. So long as the emperor's
purse was full and his mind entertained with shows
and plays he did not meddle with their deeds.
Weak, wicked, and foolish as he was himself,
Claudius is most notorious for the wives that shared

his throne and surpassed his
misdeeds. Messalina, his
first empress, was so utterly
bad that her name has
passed into current lan-
guage as a synonym of fem-
inine licentiousness. She
was unfaithful to her husband and murdered her
rivals and her enemies.

Messalina.

Narcissus at last gained
the emperor's consent to have her killed. Agrippina, his niece and second wife, was scarcely an

improvement. Though she did not flaunt her immoralities in public, like Messalina, she was quite as unscrupulous and thoroughly bad. Claudius had two children by Messalina, Britannicus and Octavia ; but Agrippina persuaded him to adopt her own son, Nero, for whom she coveted the throne. Nero was married to Octavia, and Britan-

Agrippina.

nicus was shoved aside in the bestowal of favors. When her plans were ripe the empress poisoned her husband (54 A. D.). The reign of Claudius yielded but few events of public importance. The conquest of Britain was undertaken and the southern portion formed into a province. In general the empire was quiet and prosperous. "The empire is peace" became a proverb, and it is prob-

Nero. Fifth Emperor (54-68 A. D.).

ably true that, although the personal iniquities, persecutions, and extortions of Tiberius, Caligula, and Claudius were heavily felt in Rome and Italy, the great part of the empire was well-governed, and Roman law and the Latin language were extended every-where about the Mediterranean.

Agrippina succeeded in seating her son Nero
in the chair of the Cæsars. Burrhus, the commander of the Prætorian Guard, was on her side,
and the Senate and the friends of Britannicus
yielded with enforced grace. It was several years before the character of the young ruler became known.
His mother for a time directed the affairs of State
and left him to his school-masters, and to the music and drama in which he especially delighted.
Augustus had been a conscientious ruler, Tiberius's
reign had been darkened by the horrors of its
closing years, Caligula and Claudius were quite
incapable of government, and charitable observ-
ers excuse their grievous blunders on the plea of
insanity. But for Nero, the last of the five Julian
emperors, no such excuse can be made. His guard-
ians, the honest soldier Burrhus and the philoso-

Seneca.

pher Seneca, did their best to
prepare him for his duties.
The young man delighted in
music, painting, poetry, and the
drama. In fact, he cared more
for the stage than for the State.
He acted in the public theaters
and compelled dignified senators to degrade themselves to
the same level. No favorite
was strong enough to control
this emperor. His cruelty was boundless. He
pushed aside his old teachers and had his own
mother murdered, his half-brother, Britannicus,

poisoned, and his wife, Octavia, disgraced. His second wife, the beautiful Poppæa Sabina, died from a kick which he gave her in an angry fit. In 64 A. D. a great fire swept for six days through the most crowded portions of Rome. Men said—how truly we cannot tell—that the flames had been spread by the emperor's orders, and that he

Poppæa Sabina.

viewed the scene from his palace roof, fiddling merrily and reciting Homer's description of the burning of ancient Troy. Such rumors were uncomfortable, and the generally disliked and distrusted Christians were accused of the incendiarism. Thus arose the first persecution of the Christians (64 A. D.), upon which Nero lavished his artistic cruelty in devising new modes of torture and execution. The burnt district was claimed as public property and laid out on a magnificent scale with parks, gardens, and public building. On his own new palace, the "Golden House," he expended the revenues of a kingdom. Such extravagance and such cruelty were unheard of. The provinces suffered from the taxes necessary to supply the emperor's purse, and the empire was depleted of its greatest men to satisfy his fierce and suspicious moods. Burrhus and Seneca, the guides of his youth, Lucan, the poet, Pætus, the

13

noblest of the senators, Corbulo, the greatest of
his generals, met death at his orders.   Conspiracies began to gather at Rome to rid the realm of
this monster of crime.   Vindex, a Gaulish chief-
tain, roused his countrymen against the Roman

 misrule.   At the same time Sul-
picius Galba, the Roman gov-
ernor of Spain, was hailed as
imperator by his soldiers, and
set out for Rome.   Nero had
no troops with which to defend
himself, for his prætorians
were sick of him and refused
to obey his orders.   He fled
from his palace to the home of
one of his former slaves.   The
Senate boldly declared him an

Galba.   Sixth Emperor
(68-69 A. D.).

outlaw and set a price upon the Cæsar's head.   At
the news he killed himself (68 A. D.).   With the
death of Nero expired the Julian line of emperors—the descendants by adoption of the family of
Julius Cæsar and Augustus.   The names Augustus
and Cæsar became titles, which each Roman emperor bore without respect to his family connection.

The next twelve rulers of Rome may be divided,
for convenience of memory, into four triads :
Three legionary emperors, three Flavian emperors, three statesmen, and three Antonines.

The three legionary emperors, Galba, Otho, and
Vitellius, owed their elevation to the soldiers.
Galba was proclaimed emperor by his troops in

Spain, and with them marched to Rome. Nero was dead and the servile Senate conferred the imperial offices and honors upon Galba. The new

Otho. Seventh Emperor (69 A. D.).

Vitellius. Eighth Emperor (69 A. D.).

emperor was seventy-three years old, and completely under the rule of unprincipled favorites. Otho, a senator, and former boon companion of Nero in his wild dissipations, conspired against him and won the favor of the prætorians. The aged emperor attached a young noble, Piso, to himself as colleague; but this could not save him. The guards proclaimed Otho emperor and killed both Galba and his colleague (69 A. D.). There were other legions than those in Spain and other popular men than Galba and Otho. The Roman army on the Rhine marched to Italy to place its leader, the drunken and gluttonous Vitellius, in Cæsar's seat. Otho was an incompetent general, but the prætorians were faithful to him ; the legions on the Danube and those in Syria under Vespasian were also loyal. If they could reach Italy in time he might be safe. But the army of Vitellius was the first to pass the Alps. Otho's miserable force of prætorians, marines and gladiators was routed at Cremona, and the emperor of a few months took his own life. Vitellius allowed his legions to plunder and outrage as they pleased on the southward march to the capital. In Rome the unhesitating Senate honored this red-faced reveler with the dignity of Augustus. It is to the honor of Rome that this man—the worst of her rulers—remained in power but a few months. From the Danube and the East came the succors which Otho had summoned. Antonius, with the vanguard, defeated the generals of Vitellius and captured Rome. The dissolute emperor was dragged from a dog-kennel, his hiding-place, and roughly slain. The reigns of these three legionary emperors, Galba, Otho, and Vitellius, aggregate but a little more than a single year (68–69 A. D.).

Vespasian.
Ninth Emperor (69–79 A.D.).

Vespasian — Titus Flavius Vespasianus was his full name —had no better title to the throne than had the three legionaries who preceded him. There was no Julian blood in his veins, nor had he been adopted into the imperial family. His ancestry was obscure. Some said his great-grandfather was a farm hand. Surely his father was a tax-gatherer or something of that sort. In Nero's reign Vespasian had served with credit in the army and as a capable provincial governor, but he had none of the courtier's graces, even falling asleep at the theater while the emperor acted on the stage, and was no favorite with the conceited monarch. The terrible revolt of the Jews (66 A. D.) called for Rome's best general, and Vespasian was sent to Judæa to re-conquer the country. He took with him his elder son, Titus, leaving behind him at Rome his brother Sabinus and his younger son, Domitian. The Judæan war was prolonged by the stubborn resistance of Jerusalem, and Vespasian was still in Syria when the news of the usurpations of Galba, Otho, and Vitellius reached him. His son, his friends, and his soldiers pressed him to claim the empire for himself. He yielded, and went to Rome, which the troops of Antonius had already captured in his name. The Gauls and Germans had risen in insurrection under Civilis, but Vespasian's General, Cerealis, subdued the dangerous rising (71 A. D.). Titus, who had been left in Judæa, brought the three years' siege of Jerusalem to an end (70 A. D.). The Romans were exasperated by the rigors of this war; and the Jews fought madly after their walls were scaled. The city was given over to pillage, burnings, and slaughter ; blood ran in the streets, the magnificent temple was destroyed so that not one stone was left upon another. Never was prophecy more strikingly fulfilled than in this destruction of

Jerusalem. In his splendid triumphal procession at Rome Titus exhibited the spoils of the temple—the golden candlestick and the sacred vessels, and a representation of these may still be seen carved upon the Arch of Titus at Rome which commemorates the fall of the Jewish capital.

Vespasian was a good emperor. In contrast to the Julian line, he was simple in taste, mild in temper, frugal in his habits of life. His economies and new means of raising revenue re-filled the empty treasury. Men said that he loved money too well; but his money was honestly gained and wisely expended for the improvement of the city. He died in the tenth year of his reign (79 A. D.), after a long and honorably-spent life.

Titus, the second of the Flavian family, suc-

ceeded to his father's place. Indeed, during Vespasian's lifetime this energetic son had been admitted to a large share in the Government. To his liberal policy are due some of the finest monuments of Roman architecture which have survived. The Arch of Titus stands almost intact. The enormous Flavian Amphitheater,

Titus. Tenth Emperor (79-81 A. D.).

where gladiatorial shows were given to please the populace, is the greatest of ancient ruins. The colossal statue which adorned this building gave it the name Colosseum by which we know it. The massive strength of the building inspired the lines :

"While stands the Colosseum Rome shall stand;
When falls the Colosseum Rome shall fall;
And when Rome falls—the world!"

Titus ruled the empire alone for only two years (79–81 A. D.), but he gained the affection of his subjects and was sincerely mourned at his death. The reign is notable for a great fire at Rome, a devastating plague in Italy, and a series of earthquakes in Campania, followed by the most famous disaster in history—the eruption of Vesuvius (79 A. D.). For hundreds of years the volcano had been inactive. The cities of Pompeii and Herculaneum nestled at its foot, and were favorite places of resort for wealthy Romans. Suddenly the volcanic forces in the mountain were let loose. Ashes and molten stones poured from the crater and fell upon the country round. The inhabitants of Pompeii and Herculaneum fled with what haste they could. Many were struck down by cinders, suffocated by gases, or imprisoned forever in the houses and temples where they sought shelter. The younger Pliny, who witnessed the scene from a ship in the Bay of Naples, gives a graphic description of its wonders in his famous letters. His uncle, Pliny the Elder, the famous

Pliny, the Younger.

naturalist, went ashore to study the phenomenon; but his devotion to science cost him his life.

Vespasian and Titus were well advanced in life

Domitian. Eleventh Emperor (81–96 A. D.).

when they came to power, and the elevation did not make their hard heads dizzy. Domitian was only a boy when the good fortune of his father, Vespasian, made him an emperor's son. During the reigns of his father and brother the wild young prince was kept in check ; to cover his real character he assumed the cloak of idiocy, filling the mouths of the gossips with stories of his fly-killing exploits. He came to the throne in 81 A. D. For a few years his rule was just and gentle, like that of the other Flavians, but his personal cowardice in the wars which he undertook led to conspiracies against him, and his costly and fruitless campaigns emptied his coffers. To protect himself and to replenish his treasury he exerted all his despotic power. His murders and his confiscations were as numerous and as unprovoked as those of the worst of his predecessors. He trusted no one, and those philosophers and Christians whose theory of life raised them above the fear of death were objects of his especial dread. Such he cruelly persecuted. His own wickedness and his failure as a soldier made him jealous of the good and brave.

Agricola, who had conquered the greater part of Britain, was a notable victim of his distrust. Members of his own household were not above his suspicion. Even his wife discovered that he had determined upon her death. But she forestalled his purpose and had him murdered in his palace (96 A. D.). Agricola's conquest of Britain is the sole glory of his reign. Elsewhere the Roman armies were defeated, and on the Danube they had to buy peace of the Dacians by a yearly tribute to their king, Decebalus.

Nerva. Twelfth Emperor (96-98 A. D.).

The commander of the Prætorian Guard was an accomplice of the empress in the assassination of Domitian, and helped to select the new emperor. The choice of the guard fell upon Marcus Cocceius Nerva, a senator of high character but small distinction. Nerva was accepted by the Senate and the citizens, and signalized his rule by trying to undo the wicked acts of the former reign. He repealed the laws concerning treason, which had been so abused that no wealthy citizen had been safe from the greed or malice of the informers; the political outlaws of the Flavian times were recalled, and the burdensome taxes which had been imposed by Vespasian and his successors to pay for wars and public works were reduced. Nerva died after sixteen months of power (96–98 A. D.)—long enough to give him place in the triad of "statesmen emperors."

The wisest act of the Emperor Nerva was his selection of Marcus Ulpius Trajanus to succeed

Trajan. Thirteenth Emperor (98–117 A. D.).

him. Trajan, as he is known to history, was the first Cæsar who was not Italian by birth—a fact significant of the decay of the old Roman exclusiveness. No man could have been better fitted for the task of government. A soldier of eminent abilities, he was able to preserve order within the empire, to protect its frontiers, and even to extend its boundaries. As a statesman he was liberal and prudent, and while greatly adorning the capital his care extended to every province of the empire. He was born in Spain, and it may be that this fact led him to value the provinces as highly as the capital. Trajan was with the army in Germany when his young relative, Hadrian, brought him the news of his selection by Nerva. For a year he made no haste to return to the city, although by his letters to the Senate he accepted the imperial dignity at Nerva's death. He entered Rome quietly, with his wife Plotina, like a private citizen, dwelt in frugality and simplicity in a plain house, and saved his income to expend it for public objects. The revenues of the empire were laid out in improvements which benefited all parts of the domain. The city itself was furnished with an abundant supply of pure water, which was brought from the distant hills, not in subterranean pipes, but along lofty aqueducts of stone. The theater was enlarged and remodeled for the comfort of the people. Artificial harbors were built near the mouth of the Tiber and at Ancona, on the east coast of the peninsula. Provision was made for the State support of poor orphans, and for similar purposes, which indicates the ruler's enlightened policy and his real interest in the welfare of his people.

The conspicuous statesmanship of this famous emperor was surpassed by his qualities as a soldier. Roman armies had won few laurels since the time of Augustus. In Domitian's reign they had suffered ignominious defeat. The Dacian king, Decebalus, dwelling in the mountainous region north of the Danube, now comprised in Austria-Hungary and Roumania, compelled the Romans to purchase peace with annual tribute money (90 A. D.). Trajan discontinued these humiliating payments, and the consequent dissatisfaction led to war. In 101 A. D. the Roman army, led by the emperor in person, crossed the Danube by a bridge of boats, penetrated the mountains (the Transylvanian Alps) and took the strongholds of the king. He promised submission and made peace (102 A. D.).

Three years later the war was renewed. Trajan built a massive bridge of stone near the point where the Danube breaks through the mountains (the Iron Gate). Thence by several routes his armies converged upon the Dacian forces. This time Trajan's conquest was thorough. Decebalus killed himself in the moment of defeat (107 A. D.), and his kingdom became a Roman province. Roads were built across its plains and through its mountain passes; Roman colonies were planted on its city sites, and the customs, the language, indeed the very name of Rome were impressed upon the conquered nation; for to this day the people of Dacia call themselves "Romanians," and their speech is clearly akin to the Romance tongues of Italy, Spain, and France.

On his return from Dacia the emperor celebrated a splendid triumph with the grandest gladiatorial games that the spectacle-loving populace had yet witnessed. As a monument of victory he began the erection of his forum. This was a grand public square, entered through a triumphal arch and inclosed by marble colonnades. Within it rose the famous column of Trajan, one hundred and twenty-eight feet in height. It was built of great blocks of marble, whose surface was thickly crowded with a sculptured panorama of the Dacian war. Above all was a splendid statue of the imperator. The column stands yet in its old place, the sculptures still fresh upon its surface; but the effigy of St. Paul has displaced the heathen emperor upon its summit.

The warlike emperor spent little time in his house. The camp was his home, and he found little delight elsewhere. The activity of his generals in Syria brought on a war with the once dreaded Parthians (113 A. D.), and again Trajan took personal command of his army. The Parthians were no longer the untamed race which they were two centuries before. The emperor met but weak resistance from them. He marched farther eastward than any Roman general had yet been. He visited the ruins of Nineveh, the old cities of Babylon and Susa, and reached the waters of the Persian Gulf. On his return his body yielded to the stress of long and arduous labors, and at Selinus, in Cilicia, he breathed his last (117 A. D.), naming as his successor, in almost his latest breath, that Hadrian who, twenty years before, had hurried to his camp in Gaul with the news of his own selection.

Publius Ælius Hadrianus—the Emperor Hadrian of history—proved himself a worthy successor of Trajan. His policy was a proper sequel to that of his predecessor. Trajan had advanced the limits of the empire to their widest extent; Hadrian took measures to secure the empire in its possessions. He recognized that the defense of the eastern lands which the Roman armies had lately traversed would be a killing burden, and he ac-

cordingly abandoned the conquests beyond the
Euphrates river.   Although no warrior Hadrian
was in Rome as little as Trajan had been.   His

Hadrian. Fourteenth
Emperor (117–138 A. D.).

years were passed in ceaseless
journeyings from province to
province of his empire, directing improvements, superin-
tending the defenses, and
stimulating the arts and sci-
ences.   From Gaul he crossed
to Britain, where only one
emperor, Claudius, had preceded him.   Here he pursued
his defensive policy by building the triple rampart known
as "Hadrian's Wall" across the island to protect
the Roman province from the savage Picts and
Scots of the Caledonian highlands.   In remote
parts of the empire have been found inscriptions
commemorating Hadrian's sojourn.

Like Alexander, he visited the ruins of ancient
Troy; the name of his wife is carved upon the
singing statue of Memnon in Egypt; an engraved
Algerian tablet shows that Africa was not neglected.   In Greece the emperor lingered with especial fondness.   His love for the fine arts found
gratification there and aroused a sentimental affection for Athens which Rome, his birthplace
and capital, could not inspire.   He loved to adorn
the old Hellenic city with new buildings, and under his patronage a new quarter, the City of Ha-

drian, was added to the historic town. Curiosity led him to pry into all religions and philosophies with which his journeyings brought him in contact, and he was generally tolerant of all. It is worthy of remark that he decreed divine honors to a young shepherd, Antinous, who loved him and died in his service.

Other emperors had adorned Rome with palaces; Hadrian left his tomb as his monument in the city and built his palace in the country, at Tivoli, where in the grounds about this famous villa were represented the most famous scenes of which the poets and historians had written.

Two events of the reign deserve especial mention: the codification of the laws and the dispersion of the Jews. The Roman prætors in every country acted as judges in the law-courts, and the body of decisions accumulating through the course of several centuries was now collected by an eminent lawyer, arranged in systematic shape, and published as "Hadrian's perpetual edict," to guide the decisions of future magistrates.

After the wars of Titus the Jews still looked for their Messiah. Many false prophets came, raised the standard of brief revolt and perished under the Roman sword. In 132 A. D. a new prophet, Bar Cochba, roused his Hebrew countrymen to another hopeless struggle. Hadrian had countermanded a law of Moses, and had determined to plant a Roman city, bearing his own name, upon the site of the ruined city of David. It was hopeless for the Jews to struggle against Rome, but it took the best general in the empire three years to put them down. Half a million Jews were killed in the rebellion, and the nation was made a wanderer on the face of the earth.

Toward the close of his life Hadrian became suspicious of those around him. Ælius Verus, whom he had adopted as his successor, himself preceded the emperor to the grave. His second choice fell upon Titus Aurelius Antoninus. In 138 A. D. the emperor died, and his ashes were laid in the great mausoleum which he had built at Rome on the right bank of the Tiber, and which may still be seen, massive and strong, where, as the castle of St. Angelo, it dominates the papal city.

Antoninus remained by Hadrian's bedside to soothe the last hours of his delirium, and then returned to Rome and accepted the imperial honors from the Senate. For Hadrian, the cruelties of whose last months had almost obliterated the record of his many years of moderation, the new emperor secured the divinity which the Senate would have withheld. For himself he asked nothing but received much. "Augus-

Antoninus Pius. Fifteenth Emperor (138–161 A. D.).

tus" and "Cæsar" he was by long-established
custom; but he must have treasured above all his
titles the name of "Pius," which meant at once
"the kind, the gentle, the devoted." History relates little of the life and reign of Antoninus Pius.
Few emperors reigned so long, none left so brief
a chronicle. The empire was at peace; the Dacians turned at times upon their conquerors, and
the Jews, where they could gather, struck a blow
for their despised race, but no dangerous war
ruffled the composure of the realm. The emperor
dwelt at Rome without pomp or display. He did
his duty by his family and by his subjects. The
Senate was treated with consideration, the legions
had no ground of complaint, the prætorians lay
quietly in camp without the gates. The great
public works begun by Hadrian were completed.
In Gaul, the family home of the emperor, great
buildings were erected at his charge. The empire prospered, and foreign kings and envoys
flocked to Rome to lay their disputes before a
judge so wise, so just, as the "first of the Antonines." In Rome, or at his country-seat in Etruria,
he divided his attention between the public interests and the education of the boys, Marcus
Aurelius and Lucius Verus, whom Hadrian had
recommended to his care. The former lad grew
up after his adoptive father's own heart, and
when the old man died (161 A. D.) succeeded to
the throne.

When only a little boy the manners of Marcus
14

Aurelius had caught the fancy of the Emperor Hadrian. Ælius Verus, the emperor's colleague, had

adopted him, and later at Hadrian's wish Antoninus Pius selected him as his successor. Thus the boy had the benefit of royal favor from childhood up. His tastes were scholarly, and his teachers—among them the rhetorician Fronto and the philosopher Rusticus —were worthy of their pupil. At the age of eight years the little prince was made a priest of Mars, at fifteen he

Marcus Aurelius. Sixteenth Emperor (161–180 A. D.).

was for a time governor or prefect of the city of Rome; but such premature honors did not turn his mind from study. His teachers and his own thought led him to adopt the stoic philosophy as the guide of his life—the noblest creed that the Greeks had formulated. He was a tender and affectionate father, a wise and liberal sovereign. In Marcus Aurelius monarchy vindicated itself, for the one man who was raised above his fellows as a law-giver was the one man best fitted for the elevation.

For eight years (161–169 A. D.) Marcus Aurelius and his adopted brother, Lucius Verus, occupied the throne together, but the incapacity of the latter has made him sink out of history as his dissipations hastened him out of the world. The conduct of a war of defense against the Parthians (162–165 A. D.) fell to Verus and his abler lieutenants. The latter won victories for which the pleasure-loving emperor claimed the honor of a triumph, though he had reveled at Antioch while the legions were contending with the foes of Rome. While Verus was in the East Marcus Aurelius conducted the affairs of the empire with great ability. The Senate, which, under some of his predecessors had been deprived of all share in the government, was restored to much of its republican authority. The emperor guided, but did not dictate, its legislation. From the days of the Gracchi the State had recognized its obligation to contribute to the support of the citizens. Doles of grain had been granted, with few exceptions, almost continually since that time. Further provision was made for the support of the people of Italy, who grew poorer and less numerous as their worn-out lands were deserted for more favored parts of the empire. These measures of relief and charity were extended by the Antonines, and under Marcus Aurelius officers were appointed in all parts of Italy to guard against famine by proper distribution of the foreign supply of grain.

But there was little peace for the peace-loving emperor. The empire was surrounded by enemies like a treasure-house beset by robbers. It had gathered within its boundaries all the civilized nations of the earth (save those of remote and un-

known Asia) and had thrust prosperity and civilization upon Spain, Gaul, and Britain. Within
these boundaries dwelt many races, peaceful and
happy; beyond the wall of Hadrian, the Rhine
and the Danube, were millions of men as strong
in body and as brave in spirit as any who lived
under Roman law. They had reached varying
degrees of civilization, but were all included by
the haughty Romans under the general name
barbarians. These races inhabited the whole of
central and northern Europe, and the sight of the
rich Roman provinces was ever tempting them
across the boundaries in quest of plunder or of
permanent abodes. By fortresses, by unbridged
rivers, by walls, as in Britain and in Germany between the Rhine and Danube, Rome endeavored
to protect her treasures; but it was beyond her
power to garrison and guard a thousand miles of
frontier from an ever watchful foe. In the reign
of Marcus Aurelius the peril of her position was
impressed upon her by frequent incursions from
the north. From 166 A. D. to 180 A. D. the
emperor was almost continually in the camp
of the legions, beating back the tide of German invasion that threatened Italy. The devastating plague which the Eastern army brought to
the peninsula on their return carried off his colleague Verus (169 A. D.) and left Marcus Aurelius the sole Cæsar. Of his wars on the Danube
there is not much to record. The chastisement of
one fierce tribe had no deterrent effect upon its

neighbors, and the northland swarmed with unconquered nations ready to replace the fallen.
Some were beaten to submission, others were pacified by bribes, but such arrangements could be only
temporary; the final reckoning between Rome and
the barbarians was deferred until a later century.
In the midst of his warfare the great emperor
was taken from the world by a fever. He died at
Vienna in the year 180 A. D.

Among the noblest and purest of heathen writ-
ings is the book of *Meditations*, in which this imperial philosopher wrote down his thoughts concerning life. Although great and good in his
rule, and faithful to his duty as he saw it, Marcus
Aurelius was the author of a bitter persecution of
the Christians. This "Jewish sect," as the Romans called it, was unpopular because it declined
to worship the deified emperors and refused to join
in the State festivals, which were invariably celebrated in the name of a heathen god. Nero was
the first of the persecuting emperors, but the second persecution was one of Domitian's crimes.
Trajan and Hadrian, in their zeal for good government, harried thousands of Christians to death.
Among those who suffered martyrdom under
Marcus Aurelius was Polycarp, Bishop of Smyrna,
the friend and companion of St. John the Evan-
gelist. The growth of Christianity may be
judged from the fact that the twelfth legion of
the Roman army in 175 A. D. was almost entirely
composed of Christians.

The descent from Vespasian to Domitian was not so great as from Marcus Aurelius to his degenerate son, Commodus, who succeeded to the throne at his father's death. He abandoned the care of the frontier to his officers and purchased peace where he could, for he preferred the luxury of the capital to the hardships of tent and saddle. This last of the Antonines—as we may call him, though

Commodus. Seventeenth Emperor (180-192 A. D.).

several of his successors took the name of Antoninus, in memory of the great men who had rightfully borne it—was cruel and suspicious. He feared the Senate which his father and the Flavians had respected, and its members became again the prey of his informers. The Christians went unscathed through this reign, possibly because the emperor was generally lax in his enforcement of law, or it may be on account of the influence which individual Christians gained in the palace. The disgraceful public exhibitions in which Nero displayed his artistic skill before the populace were outdone by Commodus. The latter was the more genuine Roman. Nero strove for eminence in the gentle arts of the Greeks ; Commodus sought and gained distinction in the bloody games of Rome. He won seven hundred and fifty gladiatorial contests—no great marvel, perhaps, for what poor slave would dare to flesh his sword upon a royal combatant? Lions, tigers, and elephants were brought to Rome that he might " hunt " them in the amphitheater, and he claimed the honor of slaying one hundred lions with one hundred arrows.   Like Domitian, he was slain (192 A. D.) by the men and women of his own household, who feared his cruel temper.

So ended the seventeenth Cæsar, the last of our four triads.

Ovid.

CHAPTER VIII.

THIRD PERIOD (Continued).

THE ROMAN EMPIRE.

Part II (284 years, 192–476 A. D.).

FROM THE DEATH OF COMMODUS TO THE FALL OF
THE WESTERN EMPIRE.

AT the death of Commodus the Roman Empire
was still intact. The barbarians had been beaten
or bought, and although their attacks were incessant and grievous to bear no Roman territory had
yet been relinquished. Another fact is noticeable:
although the armies on the frontier had more than
once asserted and established the right of their
own leaders to rule the empire they had not endeavored to break off fragments of the empire in
order to erect them into kingdoms. In the era
which now opens the armies became almost the
sole source of imperial power. The times of the
"legionary emperors" were re-enacted, and while
these frequent and violent changes of government
and constant civil wars sapped the military
strength of the State the barbarians on the north
increased the pressure of their advance. Thus

weakness within and dangers without threatened
the collapse of the structure.

The conspirators who had killed Commodus
were ready with a man to fill his place. They
chose a prominent member of the Senate, Pertinax, who might have proved himself an able ruler
had not the opposition of the Prætorian Guard put
an end to his reign three months after its begin-

Pertinax.   Eighteenth Emperor
(193 A. D.).

Septimius Severus.
Twentieth Emperor
(193–211 A. D.).

ning. The guards then offered the imperial honors to the highest bidder, and another senator,
Didius Julianus, was the purchaser. The price is
said to have been the payment of $1,000 to each
soldier. But the prætorians were not strong
enough to deliver the goods that they had
sold. The army in Illyria was more numerous
and better led, and now proclaimed as emperor
one of its own officers, Septimius Severus. The
armies in Gaul and the east, mindful of Vespa-

sian's victories, likewise undertook to place their
commanders on the throne of the Cæsars. With a
directness and energy suggesting the military
genius of Julius Cæsar, Septimius first marched
upon Rome. Abandoned by his purchased guards,
Didius Julianus was captured and put to death.
The prætorians were banished from Italy, and a
new Prætorian Guard of 50,000 veterans was
formed to protect the emperor's person and capital. Having taken these precautions in Italy
Severus turned upon his competitors. The eastern army was met and destroyed in Asia, and the
western found no better fate in Gaul. Thus freed
from rivalry the master of the empire led his legions to the ever-perilous frontier. In Parthia, at
one end of the line, and in Britain, in the farthest
west, he conducted successful campaigns. At
York, in Northern Britain, his life and long reign
ended, 211 A. D.

Septimius Severus left his throne jointly to his
two miserable sons, Bassi-
anus and Geta. The former
was nicknamed "Caracalla"
from the hooded great-coat
which the Gauls called by
that name and for which
the emperor set the style at
Rome. He soon became sole
Cæsar, having slain his
brother by his own hand.
Although Caracalla belongs

Caracalla. Twenty-first Emperor (211-217 A. D.)

in the list of the most infamous of the Roman emperors his reign is more memorable than that of the good Antoninus. The public baths with which he adorned the city of Rome were more extensive than those of Titus, and their ruins may still be seen. The money which was needed for this immense structure, for retaining the favor of the prætorians, and for paying the border garrisons, was obtained from the provinces by gross exactions. In order to extend the range of his tax collections the emperor extended the privileges —and the burdens—of Roman citizenship to all the free inhabitants of the empire, thus removing the last civil barrier between the mother-city and her children. The wars of his time were inglorious, and his own military ability was inconspicuous. One of his own soldiers was his murderer (217 A. D.).

For nearly one hundred years from the time of Caracalla the empire went on from bad to worse. Fully twenty emperors gained the throne within that century, commonly winning and keeping their honors by no other right than the might of their legions. Among this score were men of every grade of strength. Some may be passed in silence, others gained a horrid prominence by their misdeeds; still others showed themselves worthy of the purple. Elagabalus (218–222 A. D.), the twenty-second Cæsar, was the worst. He was a priest of the Syrian sun-worship, and was foisted upon the Romans by the eastern army. After four years of shameful living the prætorians put him to death.   Alexander Severus, his successor (222–235 A. D.), ranks among the best of the emperors.   The great lawyers Ulpian and Julius Paullus continued a work which Papinian had begun in the reign of Septimius Severus, namely, the systematic arrangement or codification of Roman law.   Under Alexander the empire was well defended ; wars were waged against the Persians, who had

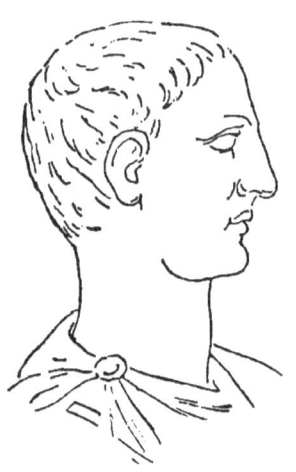

Alexander Severus. Twenty-third Emperor (222–235 A.D.).

now displaced the Parthians as the chief enemies of Rome in Asia, and against the invincible German tribes which ever refused to accept the Rhine as the boundary of the empire and resisted all attempts to Romanize their own land.   The otherwise insignificant emperor Philip (244–249 A. D.) borrows a certain importance from the thousandth anniversary of the city, which was celebrated at Rome with extravagant splendor on April 21, 248 A. D.   Under his successor, Decius (249–251 A. D.), was inaugurated a famous persecution of the long suffering Christian Church. Most of the emperors of this age fell in battle or were murdered by their soldiers.   Valerian (253–260 A. D.) was taken alive by the Persians, whose king used his living body for a horse-block and after death had his skin stuffed in the likeness of life. After Valerian's reign claimants to the purple appeared in every land. Nineteen imperators were proclaimed by the legions and strove among themselves for the supremacy. The "Age of the Thirty Tyrants" is the name by which this period goes. Such anarchy invited the Germans to fresh attacks. They came into Italy through the passes of the Alps and were well advanced on the road to the capital when Aurelian (emperor 270–275 A. D.) drove them back. For the better protection of Rome this ruler built a new wall about the capital. It was ominous of the growing peril that the imperial city could no longer depend upon its armies to hold the barbarians in check. There had been no need of a city wall since the time of Hannibal except in the civil wars. This emperor, called the "Restorer of the Universe," wisely abandoned Dacia—Trajan's conquest—whose exposed position beyond the Danube rendered it incapable of defense against the Goths who poured continually upon it from the north-east. The Syrian queen, Zenobia, of Palmyra, was conquered by this brilliant general and statesman and taken to Rome to grace his triumph.

Five emperors appeared in quick succession after Aurelian's murder, fighting each other for the throne and leading the legions against the oncoming barbarians, when it was won. In 284 A. D. a greater figure stepped out from the file of Roman rulers and took rank as a reformer and a general.

This was Diocletian. He was of humble birth, had won his military command by merit, and

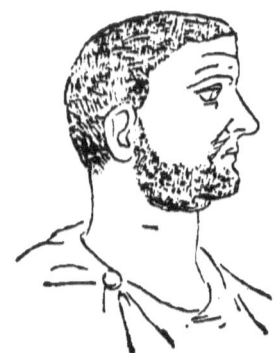

gained the imperatorship by the aid of his soldiers. As soon as his own position as Augustus was assured he voluntarily divided his honors with another commander, Maximian, who was also made Augustus. These two emperors of equal rank divided the empire, Diocletian taking the east, with his capital at Nicomedia, in Bithynia (Asia Minor), and Maximian establishing his head-quarters at Mediolanum (the modern Milan). In 293 A. D. the directing mind of Diocletian further elaborated his plan for the better government of so vast an empire. Each Augustus must now adopt a Cæsar as his successor and give him immediate, though not equal, partnership in the Government. Accordingly two Cæsars, Constantius and Galerius, were appointed, and the superintendence of the Roman world was quartered among these co-operating rulers. The four men were harmonious, and during their joint reign the empire was ably governed. Toward its close (303 A. D.) began the last and greatest persecution to which the Christians were ever subjected. The victims of death and torture numbered hundreds of thousands. The believers were outlawed, their public and private possessions

Diocletian. Forty-second Emperor (284–305 A. D.).

were taken from them, and every means was devised to exterminate the sect. Roman coins of Diocletian and Maximian have been found which commemorate the "annihilation of the Christians." In 305 A. D. the two Augusti retired to private life and the two Cæsars were raised to the full rank of Augustus. New Cæsars were created, but confusion followed. The ambition of individuals disordered Diocletian's scheme for a co-operative sovereignty. Constantine, the son of the Cæsar Constantius, assumed the title of Augustus, and the western army supported him in the assumption. Others followed his example until at one time there were six generals claiming the title of Augustus. Constantine was an energetic commander. Beginning in Britain, he fought his way to Rome, overturning his rivals and in 323 A. D. making himself sole ruler of the Roman Empire. It was in this campaign for the mastery that he saw the historic vision. A cross flamed out in the heavens as he marched, and beneath it the words *"In Hoc Signo Vinces"*—"By this sign shalt thou conquer." From that time the emperor bore the cross upon his standard, and until the fall of the empire this Christian symbol took the place of the heathen eagle which Marius had made the emblem of the Roman legions. The so-called conversion of Constantine the Great ended the persecution and raised the despised Christian faith to high honor. In 325 A. D. the emperor in person opened the first general council of the Christian

Church at Nicæa (Nice), in Bithynia.   Three hundred and eighteen bishops met in the palace and
for two months considered the interests of the
Church.   They indorsed the Athanasian theory of
Christ's divinity, denouncing the Arian heresy,
adopted the Nicene Creed, fixed the date of the
Easter celebration, and published twenty rules or
canons for the guidance of the early Church.

The edict which decreed equal rights to the
Christians is enough to distinguish the reign of
Constantine from those of his predecessors; but
another act has immortalized his name.   In 330
A. D. he removed the seat of government from the
West to the East.   Rome on the Tiber lost the
eminence which it had been achieving for eleven
hundred years, and a new Rome was founded on
the Bosphorus, where the Greek city of Byzantium
had stood for ages.   The new capital soon received
the name Constantinople—the city of Constantine.
Byzantium had been destroyed in a recent war,
and on its ruined site the emperor marked out the
plan of his proposed Christian capital.   As Peter
the Great in after times compelled the Russian
boyars to leave their ancestral homes in Moscow
and build a city of palaces in the marshes of St.
Petersburg, so Constantine compelled rich Romans
to settle in Constantinople.   His eastern subjects
gladly gathered there, and the city was soon worthy of a place of imperial residence.

The reasons for the abandonment of Rome were
various.   Constantine had determined to re-organ-

ize the Government so as to make of it an absolute despotism. The emperor was no longer to be considered the elected magistrate of a free people, and the Senate was to have no check upon him. Accordingly, Rome, with its consuls and tribunes, was left to itself, the Senate without authority, the consuls with only the government of the city in its hands. The empire was divided into four prefectures, of which Constantine appointed the governors. Furthermore these were so subdivided that the emperor was directly represented in every part of his dominions by an officer responsible to him alone. The armies were similarly subdivided in order to lessen the possibility of a grand revolt or an insurrection in favor of a popular commander. The emperor's choice was, perhaps, directed to Byzantium because that situation was in the center of the richest and most civilized part of the empire and was easily capable of defense. The natural and artificial walls which inclosed Italy were weakening before the persistent onset of the barbarians, and Rome must inevitably fall. Whatever may have been the ground for the transfer of the sovereignty, events have proved its wisdom. Before the close of the next century a barbarian chief was ruler of the city on the Tiber, but the city of Constantine remained the seat of a Roman emperor for another thousand years.

Having established with such stability as he could the despotism which he had planned, Constantine divided the realm among the members of

15

his family.   After his death (337 A. D.) his three
sons fought among themselves until 361 A. D.,
when his nephew, Julian, gained
the sole power.   He was a brave
soldier and a man of enlightened
intellect, but his attitude toward
the Christian Church gained for
him the title of "Apostate," and
has made him an object of de-
testation.   He rejected the faith
of his uncle and endeavored to
revive the worship of the old gods

Julian the Apostate.
Forty-eighth Emperor
(361–363 A. D.).

of Greece and Rome.   The effigy
of Jupiter displaced the mono-
gram of Christ on the legionary standards, and
daily sacrifice was offered in the imperial camp.
His own reverence for the ancient beliefs was
doubtless sincere, but the old stories had long since
lost their hold upon the human mind, and his elab-
orate attempts to galvanize them into life showed
their utter dissolution.   Even the books which the
apostate emperor wrote with zealous pen in order
to combat the Christian fathers are now, by the
irony of time, reckoned among the best historic
evidences of the truth of the Christian story.   After
Julian's death (363 A. D.) Christianity returned
to the empire to stay.   The histories of the time
are full of the details of the long struggle between
the creeds.   For a long time the gods remained in
the Roman temples, and the Roman Senate decreed the divinity of the deceased Augusti.   Great

calamities which befell the State were laid at the door of the Christians, and the impending dangers of barbarian invasion were variously interpreted according to the commentator's point of view.   The pagan saw in it the visitation of Jupiter's wrath upon his people for following the new faith, and the Christians declared that it was the deserved punishment of Rome for her persistent attachment to her idols.   Gradually the temples fell into neglect and Christian churches rose in the cities of the empire.   St. Sophia, at Constantinople, was one of the first and finest.   The cities were first Christianized, but the old faiths lingered long among the simple country people, the dwellers in the *pagi*, "country," or on the *haiden*, "plains," and so the words "pagans" and "heathen" came to mean the unbelievers.   Missionaries carried the Gospel across the borders of the empire to the barbarian tribes.   The Goths had the Bible in their own language in the fourth century after Christ, and many of them as well as many of the other German races accepted Christianity before they came to dwell within the limits of the empire.

About the year 375 A. D. the restlessness of the barbarian tribes was redoubled.   Behind the Germanic races which congregated on the Roman frontiers were other nations, of different blood, led on by some unexplained instinct—perhaps of plunder, possibly of conquest.   The Huns, a Turanian horde of blood-thirsty warriors, drove the milder **West Goths** (Visigoths) before them across the

Danube into Roman territory. Valens, the emperor (364–378 A. D.), allowed the latter to remain, but aferward fell in battle with them. Theodosius (emperor 378–395 A. D.) had the same West Goths to contend with nearly all his life, and when he died he divided the empire between his two sons —Honorius in the West and Arcadius in the East. Stilicho, his best general, himself a barbarian of the Vandal nation, was made protector of the lads, and when Alaric, the King of the West Goths, ravaged the provinces of Macedonia and Greece he was the only man who could stay their progress. The eastern emperor made peace with Alaric, who then attempted the conquest of Italy. Stilicho, with the army of Honorius, beat him back repeatedly (400–403 A. D.), but before he could settle with him another German horde, composed of Vandals, Suevi, and Alani, pressed into Italy under the leadership of Radagaisus. Again the great Stilicho summoned all the forces of the empire, stripping Britain, Gaul, and Spain, of their defenses. Radagaisus and his myriads were driven back, but the salvation of Italy was the loss of the western provinces. Britain was quickly overrun by the Caledonian tribes, and later by the English (Angles and Saxons) from the German sea-coast. Roman manners soon disappeared from the island. Gaul was plundered by Franks and Burgundians, and Spain was occupied by the Vandals and Suevi, from whom Stilicho's prowess had snatched Rome in a moment of desperate danger. The weak Roman

Emperor, Honorius, jealous of the general who
had twice saved Rome, had Stilicho assassinated.
The news of his death roused Alaric to another
invasion. The emperor shut himself up in his im-
pregnable fortress of Ravenna, surrounded by the
marshes of the Adriatic, and left the old capital
to care for itself. The Gothic king advanced
without opposition. No army could be gathered
in the disordered empire. The slaves flocked to
him; their masters dared not resist. For a costly
ransom he spared the city (409 A. D.), but the
next year he came again, and in August, in the
year 410 A. D., Rome was plundered by the barbarian West Goths of Alaric, as it had been sacked
by their kindred, the barbarian Gauls of Brennus,
just eight centuries previous. After twelve days
in the city the king moved southward, dying on
the march to Sicily. That no one might desecrate
the conqueror's last resting-place a stream was
turned aside for a few midnight hours and his
body was laid in a grave under its waters. His
successors, Athaulf and Wallia, made terms with
the emperor, and with his sanction founded a West
Gothic (Visigothic) kingdom in Spain and southern France, which lasted, with a few changes, for
three centuries, until the Mohammedan Arabs
from Africa conquered Spain (711 A. D.).

Although Italy was still ruled by the emperor
it was in a wretched condition, and the Western
Empire had been shorn of its provinces, Britain,
Gaul, and Spain. Africa was the next great loss.

The Vandals, who, as earlier tenants, shared the Spanish Peninsula with the Suevi and West Goths, took advantage of the civil war in the Roman province of Africa to cross the narrow seas with a powerful army and engage in the quarrel (429 A. D.). Their leader, Genseric, took the strong cities Hippo and Carthage, and the country which they defended. In the siege of Hippo died the patriotic and learned St. Augustine, the most eminent of the early "fathers" of the Christian Church. Genseric founded in Africa a Vandal kingdom which the Roman Emperor recognized as semi-independent. This Vandal State lasted a century and developed great naval power. Its swift ships, the forerunners of the Barbary pirate craft, were the terror of the western Mediterranean, whose islands, Sicily, Sardinia, and Corsica, were early captured by Vandal hands. The roughness of these barbarians, their disrespect for art and literature, has made the name of Vandal synonymous with "destroyer." In June, 455 A. D., their ruthless raids reached Rome itself. What Alaric the Goth had left of the city's possessions was taken by Genseric the Vandal. But the incursion was soon over. The barbarians retired with their spoil, leaving Italy, plundered and helpless, the easy prey of the next German horde.

In the middle of the fifth century the Huns, the fiercest of the barbarian tribes, appeared on the broken frontiers of the empire. They were a wild, rough race of Turanian origin, unlike the Germans with whom Rome had thus far come in contact. Their strange faces and unfamiliar voices deepened the terror of the impression which they made. Panic preceded their advance, and desolation followed in their train. They came from the wide grassy plains of Russia, and their first blows were at the Eastern Empire. But Constantinople was too strong for them, and, content with tributes from its ruler, they turned their eyes to easier conquests farther west. Attila, their king, known as "the scourge of God," led a vast army through the German forests into Gaul. The Germans feared him as much as did the Romans, and from their settlements he gathered great quantities of booty. Aëtius, the Roman general, massing all the available forces of the Western Empire, defeated him near Chalons, in France (451 A. D.), in the "battle of nations." This glorious victory saved Western Europe from barbarism and preserved for modern times the civilization of the Greeks and Romans. Attila's power, though checked, was not destroyed. The next year he appeared in northern Italy with a great army. The people of the fortress of Aquileia fled before him and founded Venice on the Adriatic islets. The rich cities of the Po valley surrendered to him, and no force was at hand to bar the road to Rome. But the supplications of the citizens, their rich bribes, and perhaps the expected return of Aëtius from Gaul altered the plans of the Huns. Rome was spared, and Attila, laden with booty, returned to his northern forests, where he died (453 A. D.), without establishing a permanent kingdom. The Huns soon disappear from history.

The Western Empire had now lost all its provinces, and its emperor was really subject to the Vandal and Visigothic kings, who were his nominal dependents. Ravenna had supplanted Rome as the capital, and the greatest man left to the former mistress of the world was not the heathen, Cæsar, but the Christian bishop, or "pope." Rome had so long been recognized the sovereign city that it was natural for her spiritual head to be accorded the first place in Christendom. In 476 A. D. the feeble line of Roman emperors came to an end with the boy-monarch, Romulus Augustulus, whom Odoacer, a German chief who had mastered Italy, removed from the throne. This marks the fall of the Western Empire. Odoacer was appointed "patrician" of Italy by the eastern emperor, Zeno, but seems to have conducted the government as it pleased him. The subject kingdoms in which the barbarian nations had settled soon denied all connection with the government in Italy and set up for themselves. From these independent kingdoms sprang the nations of the Middle Ages, which still exist as the republics and monarchies of Western Europe. In a concluding chapter we shall trace in outline the course of the Eastern Empire to its fall in 1453 A. D.

CHAPTER IX.

CONCLUSION.

THE EASTERN EMPIRE TO ITS FALL, 1453 A. D.

THE HOLY ROMAN EMPIRE 800–1806 A. D.

THE history of Rome properly ends with the overturn of the Western Empire by the German Odoacer in 476 A. D. From that time until the time of Charlemagne (768–814 A. D.) was a period of turmoil and constant changes in the territory once ruled from Rome. In northern Gaul the Frankish king Clovis (481–511 A. D.) defeated Syagrius, the last Roman general in that region, and established a kingdom firmly with Paris as its capital. At his direction the Franks accepted Christianity. This was the German beginning of the French nation.

In Italy, Odoacer was defeated by Theodoric (493–526 A. D.) king of the East Goths, who united also for a time the West Gothic Kingdom of Spain under his authority; but after his death the union was dissolved. Spain continued under Gothic rule; but the Italian Kingdom soon yielded to two foes, Belisarius and the Lombards. The former was the general of Justinian, the Emperor of the East (527–565 A. D.). He was one of the greatest of military leaders. So long as he lived the boundaries of the Eastern Empire were ably defended, and an attempt was made to regain the provinces which Rome had lost. The Vandal Kingdom in Northern Africa was swept up by the new wave of imperial conquest, and Italy was again included in the domains of the empire. But the Langobards (Lombards), a late arrival from the inexhaustible German forests, now came into Italy and established a Lombard kingdom on the ruins of the East Gothic, easily ridding themselves of the representatives of the Greek Empire whom Belisarius had left in Italy to govern his conquests. By degrees all Italy became Lombard, and all the Lombards became Catholic Christians. Their kingdom was absorbed (774 A. D.) by Charlemagne, King of the Franks. It was during their supremacy in Italy that the Pope of Rome, Gregory I., advanced to a position of supremacy among the bishops of the Church.

So much for the barbarian kingdoms into which the West had fallen. Meanwhile how had the East been faring? Constantinople had approved the wisdom of its founder. Wealth and population gravitated to it as their proper center. The splendid court which the emperors established there was the resort of the best minds of the Orient. The language of the city was Greek, and in its libraries and museums were assembled the finest products of Greek art and literature. While

the West was overrun by barbarian nations, ignorant and half-civilized at best, the East continued
to cultivate the learning of the ancients and the
Christian doctrines of more recent origin. Thus
the city of Constantine escaped the dark ages
through which Europe passed before the renas-
cence of Greek ideas. Although the Eastern Empire was comparatively safe from the inroads of
the German nations, it was exposed to the wild
forces which the advent of the warrior-prophet
Mohammed let loose in Arabia in the seventh century. We have already seen how Belisarius won
back Italy for Justinian, and how much of this
re-conquest was lost to the Lombards. After Justinian's death the limits of the empire shrank still
more. A few districts in Italy, the Balkan peninsula and Asia Minor obeyed the ruler at Constantinople; but that was all. The successors of Mohammed, the prophet, beginning in Arabia, conquered all the lands on the southern shore of the
Mediterranean—Syria, Persia, Egypt, Africa. Almost all these Arab gains were losses to the Greek
Empire. The imperial possessions in Europe were
at the same time fading away before the Slavonic
races, and the Turanian Bulgars and Magyars
who fastened upon the Balkan peninsula and occupied Macedonia and Greece in the seventh and
eighth centuries. Gradually the lines closed in
upon the new Rome of Constantine. The Turks,
more cruel and less enlightened, took up the Ara-
bian career of conquest in the tenth century, and

wrested the greater part of Asia Minor from the Greeks. Their cruelties to the Christians of the East brought on the Crusades, those seven wonderful wars of the cross, in which the kings and knights of Western Europe engaged during the eleventh, twelfth, and thirteenth centuries. Thanks to the German, French, and English soldiers, the Turks were kept too busy, for three hundred years, to complete the reduction of Constantinople, still the seat of empire.

With the end of the Crusades came a new peril. The Ottomans, a fresher and fiercer Mongol race than their predecessors, came into Asia Minor from the far East and swept all before them. Passing by Constantinople for the time being, they crossed into Europe and conquered the Slavs of the Balkan peninsula. The sudden irruption of Tamerlane and four hundred thousand Tartars from Central Asia saved Europe for half a century. The Turks and Tartars tried conclusions in Asia Minor, and the latter won. But Tamerlane's power did not survive his death. The Ottomans soon recovered strength and again pressed upon Constantinople. The emperor begged the Western princes to assist him, pleading the cause of Christ against the Mohammedan; but the Christian Church had long since split in two. The Church of Rome denounced the Greek Church as heretical, and all efforts to reunite the two divisions failed. Constantinople was left unaided except by a few thousands of Venetians and Genoese.

These few defenders held out for two months against the besiegers, but on the 29th of May, 1453 A. D., the city fell. Constantine XII., the last of the Eastern emperors, was killed in the final onslaught. The fall of the city of Constantine brought down with it the last vestige of the Eastern Empire. From that day until this the splendid city on the Bosphorus has been the capital of the degraded Turks.

Thus we have traced the course of the united empire to its division, 395 A. D., and the divided empires to their respective dissolutions (476 A. D. and 1453 A. D.). Here this history would naturally close were it not thought well to trace in outline the origin and existence of the "Holy Roman Empire;" a peculiar revival of the first empire by the Germans, which lasted, in name, at least, until the beginning of our own century.

The German kingdom of the Franks which Clovis founded (486 A. D.) was destined to perform a leading part in the later history of Europe. Its kings, or the ministers who governed for them, were generally able men, eager for conquest and fierce in battle. They extended the Frankish rule over a part of Germany and over almost the whole of what is now the French Republic. In the battle of Tours (732 A. D.) their general, Charles Martel, turned back the Arab conquerors of Spain, who had threatened to spread the Mohammedan religion over Western Europe. The Frankish king, Charles the Great (Charlemagne or

Karl der Grosse), one of the ablest monarchs that
ever lived, led the Franks to brilliant conquests.
The whole of France, Belgium, Switzerland, and
the Netherlands, Eastern Germany, and Austria,
and the Lombard kingdom in Italy, were brought
under his immediate control. He was a Roman
Catholic, and exerted himself to protect the interests of the Church.

On Christmas Day, in the year 800 A. D., the
Roman Pope, Leo III., solemnly crowned this
German king as Emperor of Rome. There had
been no emperor in Italy since 476 A. D., nor any
imperial authority save that which was weakly
exerted from Constantinople; but Charlemagne
assumed the style of Cæsar (*Kaiser* in the German
form), and left the imperial title to his successors.
His descendants, who divided his possessions by
the treaty of Verdun (843 A. D.), were the real
founders of the French and German nations, for
the separation of the Franks exposed the eastern
wing of that German race to the Latin influences
which were strong in Gaul since the time of
Julius Cæsar. Here the West Franks became
Latinized, and the French language took shape
out of the old German and Latin elements. On
the other hand, the East Franks, on the right bank
of the Rhine, which had never been thoroughly
subject to Rome, clung to their early speech—the
German—and still retain it. The Angles and
Saxons who crossed to Britain also retained their
Germanic language, driving out the Romanized

Britons. In Spain and Italy the Goths, Lombards and other Germanic tribes yielded to Roman influences and lost their own language in the Spanish and Italian, which are akin to French, and are classed with it as the Romance or Latinic tongue.

The Holy Roman Empire, which Charlemagne founded was revived by Otho the Great (962 A. D.), and continued to exist in *title* for a thousand years. The emperors were German kings who went to Rome only to receive the blessing of the pope. As Rome had ruled the world, so in theory the whole of Christendom formed one empire of many kingdoms, over which the German emperor and the Roman pope were jointly sovereign. In practice, however, the emperor had little authority outside of his especial dominions, which were usually limited to Germany. The kingdoms, Spain, France, and England, were independent of the emperor, and frequently more powerful than he. In the fifteenth century the succession to the imperial throne became fixed in the family of Hapsburg, the dukes of Austria. Under them the empire declined. It was a conglomeration of self-governing principalities, duchies, kingdoms, and counties, without unity of feeling and incapable of concerted action. Single States, like Austria, Bohemia, and Prussia, achieved a certain prominence, but the Holy Roman Empire was a lifeless thing. Under the pressure of Napoleon it fell in pieces. The Archduke of Austria retained the empty title of Kaiser (Cæsar) until August 6, 1806, when he abandoned the name and empty authority of Roman Emperor and assumed the new style "Emperor of the Hereditary Austrian Estates." The Holy Roman Empire has never been revived. It never was "Roman" except in name.

Domitius Corbulo.

PRONUNCIATION OF PROPER NAMES AND LATIN WORDS.

A-chæ'an (-kē').
A-chä'i-a (-kä').
Ac'ti-um.
Ad'du-a.
A'di-ge (ä'de-jä).
A-dri-ät'ic.
Æ'dile.
Æ-gē'an (-jē').
Æ-gu'sæ.
Æ'li-a Cap-i-tŏ-lī'na.
Æ-mǐl'i-us.
Æ-mil-i-ā'nus.
Æ-nē'as.
Æ'qui.
A-ē'ti-us.
Æt'na (Et').
Æ-tō'li-an.
A-frä'ni-us.
Af-ri-cā'nus.
A'ger pub'li-cus.
A-gric'o-la.
Ag-ri-gĕn'tum (-jĕn').
Ag-rip'pa.
Ag-rip-pī'na.
A-hü'la.
A-hen-o-bär'bus.
Al'a-ric.
Al'ba Lŏn'ga.
Al-ex-än'der.
A-lex-an'dri-a.
Al-gē'ri-a (-jē').
Al'li-a.
Al-lŏb'ro-ges (jēs).
Am-i-ter'num.
A-mū'li-us.
An-cō'na.
An'cus Mar'tĭ-us.
An-cy'ra (-sī').
A'ni-o.
An-tīn'o-ous.
An'ti-och (-ok).
An-tī'o-chus (kus).
An'ti-um.
An-to-nī'nus Pī'us.
An-tō'ni-us.
An'to-nīnes.
Ap'en-nines.
Ap'pi-us Clau'di-us.
A'quæ Sex'ti-æ.
Aq-ui-lē'i-a.
Ar'ab.
A-rä'bi-an.
Ar-chē'lā-us (-ke-).
Ar-mǐn'i-us.
A-rī'ci-a.
A-rim'i-num.

16

Ar'nus.
Ar-pī'num.
Ar-rē'ti-um.
Ar'sa.
Ar'si-a.
Ar'yan.
As'cu-lum.
A-si-at'ic (-shē-).
A-thaulf'.
Ath'ens.
Ath'e-sis.
A-tīl'i-us.
At'ti-ca.
At'ti-la.
Au'fi-dus.
Au-gǔs'ta Tau-rin-ō'rum
Au-gus'ti-lis.
Au-gǔs'tine.
Au-gǔs'tu-lus.
Au-gǔs'tus.
Au-rē'li-us.
Au-rē'li-an.
Av'en-tine.

Bab'y-lon.
Baj'a-zet.
Bal-kän'.
Bä'i-æ.
Bar'ca.
Bar Coch'bar (Cŏk').
Bas-si-ä'nus.
Bĕl'gi-um (ji).
Bel-i-sä'ri-us.
Ben-e-vĕn'tum.
Bi-thyn'i-a.
Bo-ad-i-cē'a.
Bœ ō'ti-a (Bē-ō'she-a).
Bo-hē'mi'a.
Bo-nō'ni-a.
Bos'pho-rus.
Bo-vi-ā'num.
Brĕn'nus.
Brit-tan'i-cus.
Brun-dis'i-um.
Brū'tus.
Brǔt'ti-um.
Bur'rhus.
By-zan'tine.
By-zan'ti-um.

Cæ'li-an (Sē').
Cæ're (Sē').
Cæ'sar (Sē'zar).
Cā'i-us
Ca-lā'bri-a.
Cal-e-dō'ni-a.

Ca-lǐg'u-la.
Ca-mǐl'lus.   [ya].
Cam-pagn'a (Käm-pän'-
C am-pä'ni-a.
Căm'pus.
Ca'naan.
Căn'næ.
Can-u-lē'i-an.
Ca-nū'si-um.
Cā'to.
Cap'it-o-line.
Cā'pri (prē).
Cā-put
Car-a-căl'la.
Car'bo.
Ca-rī'næ.
Cär'rhæ.
Car'thage.
Car-tha-gin'i-an (-jǐn').
Cas'pi-an.
Cas'si-us.
Cas'tor.
Căt'a-na.
Cat-i-lī'na.
Cat-i-lǐn-ā'ri-an.
Cat'i-line.
Ca-tǔl'lus.
Căt'u-lus.
Cau'ca-sus.
Cau'dine.
Cau'di-um.
Cĕlts (Sĕlts).
Cel-ti-bē'ri-an (Sĕl).
Cen-tu-rī-ā'ta (Sĕn).
Ce-re-ā'lis (Sē-).
Cē'rēs (Sē').
Chær-o-næ'a (Kĕr-).
Chä-lons' (Shä-lŏn').
Chär-le-mägne'   (Shär-
le-män').
Cǐ'ce-ro (Sis).
Cǐ-lǐc'i-a (Sǐ-).
Cil'ni-us (Sǐl').
Cim'ber (Sǐm').
Cim'bri (Sǐm').
Cin-cin-nä'tus (Sin-).
Cis-al-pī'na (Sis-).
Cis-äl'pine (Sis-).
Cǐ-vī'lis (Sǐ-).
Clau'di-us.
Cle-o-pä'tra.
Clo-ā'ca.
Clō'di-us.
Clō'vis.
Clu'si-um.
Cnē'i-us (Nē'yǔs).

Coc-cĕ′i-us (sĕ′).
Cŏ′clĕs.
Co-los-sĕ′um.
Co-mi′ti-a.
Co-mi′ti-um.
Còm′mo-dus.
Con′stan-tine.
Con-stan′ti-us.
Con-stan-ti-nŏ′ple.
Cor′bŭ-lo.
Cor′do-va.
Cor-fin′i-um.
Cor′inth.
Cŏ-ri-o-lā′nus.
Cor-nē′li-a.
Cor-nē′li-us.
Cor′si-ca.
Cras′sus.
Crem′e-ra.
Cre-mō′na.
Crète.
Crŏ′ton.
Cu′mæ.
Cu-inæ′an.
Cunc-tā′tor.
Cu′rĕs.
Cu-ri-ā′ta.
Cu′ri-æ.
Cu-ri-ā′ti-i.
Cu′ri-o.
Cu′rule.
Cy-nos-ceph′a-læ (Sy-).

Dă′ci-a (-shē-a).
Dan′ube.
Da-ri′us.
De-cĕb′a-lus (-sĕb′).
De-cĕm′virs (-sĕm′).
Dec′i-mus (Dĕs′)
De′ci-us (shi-).
De-lä-to′res.
Del′phī.
De-mos′the-nes.
Den-tā′tus.
Di-ā′lis.
Did′i-us.
Di-o-clē′ti-an.
Di-o-ny′sus.
Dol-a-bĕl′la.
Do-mi′ti-an.
Do-mi′ti-us.
Drĕp′a-num.
Dru′sus.
Du-il′i-us
Dyr-rā′chi-um (kï-).

Ec′nŏ-mus.
El-a-gāb′a lus.
El′ba.
E-gÿ′ri-a (je′).
E-pi′rus.
Eq′ui-rĕs.
Eq′ui-tum.
Es′qui-line.
E-trū′ri-a.
E-trŭs′can.
Eu-phrā′tes.
Eu-rym′e-don.

Eux′ine.
Ex-arch′ate (ark′).

Fā′bi-an.
Fā′bi-us.
Fas′cĕs (Fas′seez).
Fē′lix.
Fe-ti-ā′lĕs.
Fi-dē′næ.
Flăc′cus.
Flā′men.
Flam-i-ni′nus.
Fla-min′i-us.
Flā′vi-an.
Flā′vi-us.
Fŏ′rum.
Fre-gĕl′læ.
Fren-tā′ni.
Fren′to.
Fron-to.

Ga-bin′i-an.
Gal-ā′ti-an.
Gal′ba.
Ga-lē′ri-us.
Gal′lic.
Ga′vi-us.
Gĕn′o-a (Jĕn′).
Gen′o-ese.
Gĕns (Jĕnz).
Gen′ser-ic (Jen′).
Ger-măn′ic (Jer′).
Ger-măn′i-cus.
Gĕ′ta (Jĕ′).
Glăd′i-ā′tor.
Glau′cl-a.
Gŏths.
Gŏth′ic.
Grac′chi (kĭ).
Græc′chus (kŭs).
Grē′ci-an.

Hä′dri-an.
Ha-mil′car.
Hăn′ni-bal.
Ha-rŭs′pice.
Has′dru-bal.
Hel-lŏ′nĕs.
Hel-lĕn′ic.
Her-a-clē′a.
Her-cu-lā′ne-um.
Her′mann.
Her′ni-cī (-si).
Hi′e-ro.
Hi-e-rŏn′y-mus.
Ho-nŏ′ri-us.
Ho-rā′ti-i.
Ho-rā′ti-us.
Hor-tĕn′si-an.

I-a-pyg′i-an (pij′).
I-hē′rus.
Il′i-ad.
Il-lyr′i-an.
In′do-Eu-ro-pe′an.
In′ter-rĕ-gĕs (-jĕz).
I ŏ′ni-an.
Isth′mi-an.

It-al′i-an.
It-al′i-ca.
It′-a-ly.

Ja-nic′u-lum.
Jā′nus.
Je-ru′sa-lem.
Ju-dæ′a.
Ju-gur′tha.
Ju-gur′thine.
Ju′li-an.
Ju-li-ā′nus.
Ju′li-us.
Ju′ni-us.
Ju′no.
Ju′pi-ter.
Jus-tin′i-an.

Kai′ser.

Lä-bi-ē′nus.
La′rĕs.
Lăt′in.
Lā′ti-um.
La-vin′i-um.
Leg′horn.
Lĕp′i-dus.
Leu-còp′e-tra.
Lib′y-an.
Li-cin′i-us (-sin′).
Li-gŭ′ri-a.
Lil-y-bæ′um.
Lip a-ræ.
Li′ris.
Līv′i-a.
Līv′i-us.
Liv′y.
Lŏ′cri.
Lom′bard-y.
Lŭ′ca.
Lŭ′can.
Lu-ca′ni-a.
Lu′ce-res (se-).
Lu-crē′ti-a.
Lu-cŭl′lus.
Lŭ′cu-mo.
Lu-si-tā′ni-a.
Lu-tā′ti-us.

Măc′e-don (Măs′).
Mac-e-dŏ′ni-a (Mas).
Mā′cra.
Mā′cro.
Mæ-cē′nas.
Mæ′li-us.
Ma-gĭs′ter   Eq′ui-tum
(-gis′.)
Mag′na Græ′ci-a.
Măg′nŏ′si-a.
Măg′nus.
Mā-go.
Măl′ta (Mawl′).
Ma-nil′i-a.
Ma-nil′i-us.
Mŏn′li-us.
Man′tu-a.
Mar-cĕl′lus.
Mar′cus.
Mā′ri-us.

Mā'ro.
Mar'sĭ.
Mar'ti-us
Mar-tel'.
Mas-si-nis'sa.
Max-ĕn'ti-us.
Max-im'i-an.
Max'i-min.
Max'i-mus
Me-di-o-la'num.
Med-i-ter-rä'ne-an.
Mem'mi-us.
Mém'non.
Mes-sa-li'na.
Mes-sä'na.
Mes-si'na (-sē').
Met-a-pŏn'tum.
Me-tau'rus.
Me-tel'lus.
Mil'an.
Mī'lo.
Min'ci-us.
Mi-ner'va.
Min-tur'næ.
Mi-sē'num.
Mith-ri-dä'tēs.
Mith-ri-dăt'ĭc.
Mo-ham'med.
Mon'gol.
Mons Sa'cer (ser).
Mu'ci-us.
Mum'mi-us.
Mŭn'da.
Muni-cip'i-a (sĭp')
Mu-ti'na.
My'.æ.

Nä'-ples (plz).
Nar-cis'sus (sis')
Nar'ni-a.
Nar'sēs.
Nä'so.
Ne-ap'o-lis.
Nep'tune.
Nē'ro.
Ner'va.
Neth'er-lands.
Nice.
Ni-cæ'a (sē).
Nie'buhr (Nē'boor).
Nin'e-veh
Nō'la.
Nor-bä'nus.
Nu-măn'ti-a.
Nu'ma Pom-pil'i-us,
Nu-mĭd'i-a.
Nu'mi-tor.

Oc-ta-vi-ā'nus.
Oc-ta'vi-a.
O-dō'a-cer (sĕr)
O-gŭl'ni-an.
Op'ti-mates.
Or-chŏm'e-nus (kŏm').
Os'can.
Os'man.
Os'ti-a.
Os'tro-goth.

O'tho.
Ot'to-man.
Ov'id.
O-vid'i-us.

Pā'dus.
Pæ-lig'ni.
Paes'tum.
Pæ'tus.
Pàl'a-tine.
Pal-a-ti'nus.
Pa-le-ol'o-gus.
Pal'es-tine.
Pal-mv'ra.
Pan-nŏ'ni-a.
Pa-nor'mus.
Pä'ri-an.
Par'thi-an.
Pa-tri'ci-an (-trish'yan).
Pa-tä'vi-um.
Pa-vi'a (-vē').
Pel'o-pon-nē'sus.
Pe-nä'tes.
Per'ga-mon.
Per'i-cles.
Per'se-us.
Per'ti-nax.
Pe-rū'si-a.
Pe-trē'i-us.
Phar-nä'ces.
Phar-sä'lus.
Phœ-nī'ci-a.
Phi-lĭp'pi.
Phi-lip'pic.
Pī'cēne (seen).
Pi-cē'num (sē').
Pic'tor.
Pi-ræ'us.
Pī'so.
Pla-cen'ti-a (-sen').
Plau'ti-a Pa-pir'i-an.
Ple-be'i-an.
Plin'i-us.
Plin'y.
Plo-ti'na.
Pol'lux.
Pom-pē'i-an.
Pom-pē'i-ī (anc.).
Pom-pe'i-i (pa'yēē,mod)
Pom-pē'i-us.
Pom'pey.
Pon'ti-fex.
Pon-tif'i-cēs.
Pont'i-us.
Pon'tus.
Pop-pæ'a Sa-bi'na.
Por'ci-us.
Por'se-na.
Præ-nes'te.
Præ'tor.
Præ-tō'ri-an.
Pris'cus.
Pro-per'ti-us.
Ptol'e-my (Tŏl').
Pub-lic'o-la.
Pub-lil'i-an.
Pub'li-us.
Pu'nic.

Pyd'na.
Pyr'en-ees.
Pyr'rhus.

Quæs'tor.
Quin-til'i-us.
Quin'tus.
Quin'ti-us.
Quin'que-reme.
Quir'i-nal.
Qui-ri'nus.

Răm'nēs.
Ra-vĕn'na.
Re-a'te.
Re-gil'lus (-jil').
Reg'u-lus.
Rē'mus.
Rhæ'ti-a
Rhē'a Sil'vi-a.
Rhē'gi-um (je).
Rhōdes.
Rhŏ'-di-an.
Ri-vi-e'ra (Re-ve-a'ra).
Ro-ma'ni-a.
Rom'u-lus.
Roths'child (Rŏs').
Ru'bi-con.
Rus'si-an.
Rus'ti-cus.

Sa-hel'li-an
Sa'bine
Sa-bi'nus.
Sa-gun'tum.
Sal'lust.
Sal-lust'i-us.
Sam'nites.
Sam'ni-um.
Sar-din'i-a.
Săt'urn.
Sat-ur-nī'nus.
Scæv'o-la (S-ev')
Scip'i-o (Sĭp').
Se-ja'nus.
Se-leu'ci-dæ (s'-).
Se-lī'nus.
Sem-prō'ni-us.
Sen'e-ca.
Sen-ti'num.
Sep-tim'i-us.
Ser-to'ri-us.
Ser'vile.
Ser'vi-us.
Se-vē'rus.
Sex'ti-æ.
Sex'ti-us.
Sex'tus.
Sib'yl.
Si'ci-ly (Sĭs').
Si-cil'i-an (Sil').
Si'don.
Sil'a-rus.
Sil'vi-us Pro'cas.
Si-roc'co.
Sla-vo'ni-an.
Smyr'na.
So'ci-i (she-).

Soissons (Swä-sŏng').
So-phī'a.
Spar'ta.
Spar'ta-cus.
Spo-lē'ti-um.
Spū'ri-us.
Stil'i-cho (-ko).
Su-ē'vi.
Su-hur'ra.
Sul'la.
Sul'mo.
Sul-pi'ci-us.
Su-per'bus.
Su'sa.
Sy-a'gri-us.
Syb'a-ris.
Syr'a-cuse.
Syr'i-a.

Tăc'i-tus (Tăs').
Tam-er-lane'.
Tan'a-quil.
Ta-ren'tine.
Ta-ren'tum.
Tar-pē'i-a.
Tar-pē'i-an.
Tar'quin.
Tar-quin'i-i.
Tar-quin'i-us Pris'cus.
Tel'a-mon.
Teu'to-nes.
Teu-ton'ic.
Ter-en-til'i-us.
Teu'to-burg-er.
Thap'sus.
Thēbes.
The-ŏd'oric.
The-o-dŏ'si-us.
Thes'sa-ly.
Thrăce.
Thrā'ci-an.

Tī'ber.
Ti'bur.
Ti-bē'ri-us.
Ti-bŭl'lus.
Ti-cī'nus (-sī').
Ti-gra'nes.
Ti-gra-no-cer'ta.
Ti'ti-es (Tish'yes).
Tī'tus.
Tiv'o-li.
Tra'jan.
Tra-ja'nus.
Trans-al-pi'na.
Trans-al'pine.
Tran-syl'va-ni-a.
Tras-i-mē'nus.
Trĕ'bi-a.
Tre-bō'ni-us.
Treves (Trāv)-
Tri-nā'cri-a.
Tri-ŭm'vir.
Tri-um'vi-rate.
Trī'rēme.
Tul'li-a.
Tul-li-a'num.
Tul'li-us.
Tŭ-nis.
Tu-ra'ni-an.
Tus'can.
Tus'can-y.
Tyre.

Ul'pi-us.
Um'bri-a.
Um'bro-Sa-bĕl'li-an.
U'ti-ca.
U-ti-cĕn'sis (-sĕn').

Vad-i-mō'ni-an.
Va'lens.

Val-en-tin'i-an.
Va-lē'ri-us.
Văn'dal.
Va'ri-an.
Va'rus.
Var'ro.
Văt'i-can.
Ve'i-ī (Vē'yī).
Ven-ē'ti-a.
Ven'ice.
Ver-cĕl'læ (sĕl').
Ver-gil'i-us (jil).
Vē'rus.
Ves-pa'si-an.
Ves-pa-si-a'nus.
Ves'ta.
Ve-sū'vi-us.
Vī'a Sa'cra.
Vi-en'na.
Vĭm'i-nal.
Vin'dex.
Vin-do-bō'na.
Vip-sa'ni-us.
Vir'gil (jil).
Vir-gin'i-a (jĭn).
Vir-i-a'thus.
Vis'i-goth.
Vi-tĕl'li-us.
Vol-a-ter'ræ.
Vol'sci-an (-shun).
Vol'sci (sī).
Vul-tur'nus.
Vul'tur.

Xan-thĭp'pus.
Xerx'ēs.

Za'ma.
Zĕ'la.
Ze-no'bi-a.

INDEX.

www.ingramcontent.com/pod-product-compliance
Lightning Source LLC
Chambersburg PA
CBHW020056030726
47498CB00006B/1809